William Shakespeare's
Measure for Measure
In Plain and Simple English

BookCaps™ Study Guides
www.bookcaps.com

© 2012. All Rights Reserved.

Table of Contents

About This Series

The "Classic Retold" series started as a way of telling classics for the modern reader—being careful to preserve the themes and integrity of the original. Whether you want to understand Shakespeare a little more or are trying to get a better grasp of the Greek classics, there is a book waiting for you!

The series is expanding every month. Visit BookCaps.com to see all the books in the series, and while you are there join the Facebook page, so you are first to know when a new book comes out.

Characters

VICENTIO, Duke of Vienna

ANGELO, Lord Deputy in the Duke's absence

ESCALUS, an ancient Lord, joined with Angelo in the deputation

CLAUDIO, a young Gentleman

LUCIO, a Fantastic. Two other like Gentlemen

VARRIUS, a Gentleman, Servant to the Duke

PROVOST.

THOMAS, friar

PETER, friar

A JUSTICE. ELBOW, a simple Constable

FROTH, a foolish Gentleman

CLOWN, Servant to Mistress Overdone

ABHORSON, an Executioner

BARNARDINE, a dissolute Prisoner.

ISABELLA, Sister to Claudio

MARIANA, betrothed to Angelo

JULIET, beloved by Claudio

FRANCISCA, a nun

MISTRESS OVERDONE, a Bawd.

Lords, Gentlemen, Guards, Officers, and other Attendants.

Play

ACT I

SCENE I. An apartment in the DUKE'S palace.

DUKE VINCENTIO
Escalus.

ESCALUS
My lord.

DUKE VINCENTIO
Of government the properties to unfold,
Would seem in me to affect speech and
discourse;
Since I am put to know that your own science
Exceeds, in that, the lists of all advice
My strength can give you: then no more
remains,
But that to your sufficiency as your Worth is
able,
And let them work. The nature of our people,
Our city's institutions, and the terms
For common justice, you're as pregnant in
As art and practise hath enriched any
That we remember. There is our commission,
From which we would not have you warp. Call
hither,
I say, bid come before us Angelo.

To explain the qualities needed in governing well, Would make me seem enamored with the sound of my own voice;
Since I am obliged to admit that your own knowledge Of this exceeds the limits of all advice That my strength can give you: then no more remains,
But that you put your adequacy and worth,
To work. The nature of our people,
Our city's institutions, and the methods of the courts procedures
For common justice, you're as full of Art and practice as anyone
That we can remember. Here is our commission, Which we don't want you to alter. Call forth I say, and call Angelo here.

Exit an Attendant

What figure of us think you he will bear?
For you must know, we have with special soul
Elected him our absence to supply,
Lent him our terror, dress'd him with our love,
And given his deputation all the organs
Of our own power: what think you of it?

What you think he will think of us?
For you must know, we have with all the power of our hearts and minds Chosen him to supply our absence, Lent him our terror, dressed him with our love, And given him as deputy all the instruments Of our own power: what do you think of it?

ESCALUS
If any in Vienna be of worth
To undergo such ample grace and honour,
It is Lord Angelo.

If any in Vienna are worthy
To bear the weight of such ample grace and honor, It is Lord Angelo.

DUKE VINCENTIO
Look where he comes.

Here he comes.

ANGELO
Always obedient to your grace's will,
I come to know your pleasure.

DUKE VINCENTIO
Angelo,
There is a kind of character in thy life,
That to the observer doth thy history
Fully unfold. Thyself and thy belongings
Are not thine own so proper as to waste
Thyself upon thy virtues, they on thee.
Heaven doth with us as we with torches do,
Not light them for themselves; for if our virtues
Did not go forth of us, 'twere all alike
As if we had them not. Spirits are not finely
touch'd
But to fine issues, nor Nature never lends
The smallest scruple of her excellence
But, like a thrifty goddess, she determines
Herself the glory of a creditor,
Both thanks and use. But I do bend my speech
To one that can my part in him advertise;
Hold therefore, Angelo:--
In our remove be thou at full ourself;
Mortality and mercy in Vienna
Live in thy tongue and heart: old Escalus,
Though first in question, is thy secondary.
Take thy commission.

ANGELO
Now, good my lord,
Let there be some more test made of my metal,
Before so noble and so great a figure
Be stamp'd upon it.

DUKE VINCENTIO
No more evasion:
We have with a leaven'd and prepared choice
Proceeded to you; therefore take your honours.
Our haste from hence is of so quick condition
That it prefers itself and leaves unquestion'd
Matters of needful value. We shall write to you,
As time and our concernings shall importune,
How it goes with us, and do look to know

Enter ANGELO

Always obedient to your will,
I come here to know what you need from me.

There is a kind of written sign in your life,
That tells the observer your history
Completely. Yourself and your attributes
Are not your own so exclusively as to waste
Yourself on your virtues, they on you.
Heaven does with us as we do with torches,
Not light them for themselves; for if our virtues
Did not go before us, it would be
As if we didn't have them. Spirits are not finely
endowed
Except for fine purposes, nor does Nature ever
lend The smallest scruple of her excellence
Except when she, like a thrifty goddess, she
assumes For herself the privileges of a creditor,
Both thanks and use. But I do bend my speech
To one that already knows more than I know;
Hold therefore, Angelo:--
In our absence be in every respect myself;
Mortality and mercy in Vienna
Live in your tongue and heart: old Escalus,
Thought senior and first appointed, is your right
hand. Take your commission.

Now, my good lord,
There should be some more test of my temper
and quality, Before such a noble and great
figure Is stamped upon it.

No more evasion:
We have with a carefully considered and
prepared choice Proceeded to you; therefore
take your honors. The cause for my hasty
departure is so urgent That it takes precedence
over all other matters, and leaves unconsidered
Matters of needful value. We shall write to you,
As much as time and our business allows,

What doth befall you here. So, fare you well;
To the hopeful execution do I leave you
Of your commissions.

ANGELO
Yet give leave, my lord,
That we may bring you something on the way.

DUKE VINCENTIO
My haste may not admit it;
Nor need you, on mine honour, have to do
With any scruple; your scope is as mine own
So to enforce or qualify the laws
As to your soul seems good. Give me your hand:
I'll privily away. I love the people,
But do not like to stage me to their eyes:
Through it do well, I do not relish well
Their loud applause and Aves vehement;
Nor do I think the man of safe discretion
That does affect it. Once more, fare you well.

ANGELO
The heavens give safety to your purposes!

ESCALUS
Lead forth and bring you back in happiness!

DUKE
I thank you. Fare you well.

ESCALUS
I shall desire you, sir, to give me leave
To have free speech with you; and it concerns me
To look into the bottom of my place:
A power I have, but of what strength and nature
I am not yet instructed.

ANGELO
'Tis so with me. Let us withdraw together,
And we may soon our satisfaction have
Touching that point.

ESCALUS
I'll wait upon your honour.

And let you know how it goes with us, and will want to know What happens to you here. So, may you fare well; I leave you to the hopeful execution Of your commissions.

*But give me permission, my lord,
So that we can bring you something on the way.*

*I may be in too much of a hurry for that;
Nor do you, I promise, have to do
With any scruple; you have my same powers
To enforce or qualify the laws
As you yourself deem right.
I'll leave secretly. I love the people,
But I do not like to make a show of myself to them: Through it do well, I don't exactly relish Their loud applause and hails of acclamation;
Nor do I think that a man of safe discretion Would want it. Once again, goodbye.*

May the heavens see you safely to your purposes!

Lead ahead, and bring back happiness!

I thank you. Goodbye.

Exit

*I will want you, sir, to give me permission
To speak freely to you; it concerns me
To look into the extent of my commission and authority:
A power that I possess, but how strong and for what purpose I am not yet instructed.*

*Same with me. Let us withdraw together,
And we may soon have the satisfaction
Of talking about it.*

I'll go with you.

Exeunt

SCENE II. A Street.

LUCIO
If the duke with the other dukes come not to
composition with the King of Hungary, why
then all
the dukes fall upon the king.

FIRST GENTLEMAN
Heaven grant us its peace, but not the King of
Hungary's!

SECOND GENTLEMAN
Amen.

LUCIO
Thou concludest like the sanctimonious pirate,
that
went to sea with the Ten Commandments, but
scraped
one out of the table.

SECOND GENTLEMAN
'Thou shalt not steal'?

LUCIO
Ay, that he razed.

FIRST GENTLEMAN
Why, 'twas a commandment to command the
captain and
all the rest from their functions: they put forth
to steal. There's not a soldier of us all, that, in
the thanksgiving before meat, do relish the
petition
well that prays for peace.

SECOND GENTLEMAN
I never heard any soldier dislike it.

LUCIO

I believe thee; for I think thou never wast where
grace was said.

If the duke does not come with the other dukes
don't come to An agreement with the King of
Hungary, well then all
The dukes will attack the king.

May heaven grant us peace, but not the King of
Hungary's!

Amen.

You talk like the self-righteous pirate, that
Went out to sea with ther Ten Commandments,
but scraped
One of them out of the tablet.

Was it "Thou shalt not steal"?

Yes, that's the one he did away with.

Well, it was a commandment that was
commanding the captain and
All of his crew from performing their functions:
they set out To steal. There's not a soldier out of
all of us soldiers, that, while Blessing the food
before we eat, love for people
To pray for peace.

I've never actually heard a soldier say they
didn't like that.

I believe you; since I don't think you've ever
been present When people say grace before they

eat.

SECOND GENTLEMAN
No? a dozen times at least.

You don't think so? I have, at least a dozen times.

FIRST GENTLEMAN
What, in metre?

What, in meter?

LUCIO
In any proportion or in any language.

In any form or in any language.

FIRST GENTLEMAN
I think, or in any religion.

I think, or in any religion.

LUCIO
Ay, why not? Grace is grace, despite of all controversy: as, for example, thou thyself art a wicked villain, despite of all grace.

Yes, and why not? Grace is grace, despite all Controversies: like, for example, you yourself are an Evil swine, despite all of grace.

FIRST GENTLEMAN
Well, there went but a pair of shears between us.

Well, we're cut from the same cloth.

LUCIO
I grant; as there may between the lists and the velvet. Thou art the list.

I grant you; as there may be between the edges of the fabric and the velvet. You are the edge.

FIRST GENTLEMAN
And thou the velvet: thou art good velvet; thou'rt
a three-piled piece, I warrant thee: I had as lief be a list of an English kersey as be piled, as thou art piled, for a French velvet. Do I speak feelingly now?

*And you're the velvet: you are good velvet; you're
A piece that is piled three high, I bet: I would rather Be an edge of a coarse and wooly fabric, than be like you with your venereal disease, for being a French velvet. Are my words Hurting your feelings now?*

LUCIO
I think thou dost; and, indeed, with most painful feeling of thy speech: I will, out of thine own confession, learn to begin thy health; but, whilst I
live, forget to drink after thee.

*I think you did; indeed your words were Very painful: And since you've confessed That you have a venereal disease, I will begin drinking to your health; but
So long as I live, never drink after you for fear of catching it.*

FIRST GENTLEMAN
I think I have done myself wrong, have I not?

I think I have wronged myself, haven't I?

SECOND GENTLEMAN
Yes, that thou hast, whether thou art tainted or

Yes you have, whether you are contaminated or

free.

LUCIO
Behold, behold. where Madam Mitigation
comes! I
have purchased as many diseases under her roof
as come to—

SECOND GENTLEMAN
To what, I pray?

LUCIO
Judge.

SECOND GENTLEMAN
To three thousand dolours a year.

FIRST GENTLEMAN
Ay, and more.

LUCIO
A French crown more.

FIRST GENTLEMAN
Thou art always figuring diseases in me; but
thou
art full of error; I am sound.

LUCIO
Nay, not as one would say, healthy; but so
sound as
things that are hollow: thy bones are hollow;
impiety has made a feast of thee.

FIRST GENTLEMAN
How now! which of your hips has the most
profound sciatica?

MISTRESS OVERDONE
Well, well; there's one yonder arrested and
carried
to prison was worth five thousand of you all.

not.

*Look, look. Here comes Madam Mitigation! I
Have bought myself so many diseases under her
roof that the total come to—*

To how much?

Guess.

To three thousand dollars a year.

Yes, and more than that probably.

A French crown more.

*You always joke that I have French diseases;
but you
Are totally wrong; I'm perfectly sound and
healthy.*

*No, I wouldn't say healthy; I would say you are
sound as
Things that are hollow: your bones are hollow
from syphilis; Being so sinful has made a feast
out of you.*

Enter MISTRESS OVERDONE

*Hello there! Which of your hips has the worst
sciatica?*

*Well, well; there's a man that has been arrested
and carried
To prison that is worth five thousand of you all.*

Who's that, I pray thee?

And who is that, may I ask?

MISTRESS OVERDONE
Marry, sir, that's Claudio, Signior Claudio.

Well, sir, that would be Claudio, Mister Claudio.

FIRST GENTLEMAN
Claudio to prison? 'tis not so.

Claudio was sent to prison? It can't be.

MISTRESS OVERDONE
Nay, but I know 'tis so: I saw him arrested, saw
him carried away; and, which is more, within
these
three days his head to be chopped off.

*No, but I know it's true: I saw him get arrested,
saw Him carried away; and what's more, within
the next
Three days his head is going to be chopped off.*

LUCIO
But, after all this fooling, I would not have it so.
Art thou sure of this?

*But, after all of this joking, I don't want that to
happen.. Are you sure of this?*

MISTRESS OVERDONE
I am too sure of it: and it is for getting Madam
Julietta with child.

*I am too sure of it: and it is all because he got
Madam Julietta pregnant.*

LUCIO
Believe me, this may be: he promised to meet
me two
hours since, and he was ever precise in
promise-keeping.

*Believe me, it could be true: he promised to
meet me two
Hours ago, and he never breaks
A promise.*

SECOND GENTLEMAN
Besides, you know, it draws something near to
the
speech we had to such a purpose.

*Besides, you know, it sounds a bit like
What we were talking about earlier.*

FIRST GENTLEMAN
But, most of all, agreeing with the proclamation.

*But most of all, it's consistent with the
proclamation.*

LUCIO
Away! let's go learn the truth of it.

Come on! Let's go learn the truth.

Exeunt LUCIO and Gentlemen

MISTRESS OVERDONE
Thus, what with the war, what with the sweat,
what
with the gallows and what with poverty, I am
custom-shrunk.

*So, with the war, with the plague,
With the executions, and with poverty, I am
Out of customers.*

Enter POMPEY

How now! what's the news with you?

Hey there! What's the news?

POMPEY
Yonder man is carried to prison.

That man has been carried to prison.

MISTRESS OVERDONE
Well; what has he done?

Well; what has he done?

POMPEY
A woman.

A woman.

MISTRESS OVERDONE
But what's his offence?

But what has he done wrong?

POMPEY
Groping for trouts in a peculiar river.

Groping for trouts in a private river.

MISTRESS OVERDONE
What, is there a maid with child by him?

So what, is there a maid is with child by his doing?

POMPEY
No, but there's a woman with maid by him. You have
not heard of the proclamation, have you?

*No but there is a woman who has a maid that are standing by him. You have
Not heard of the proclamation, have you?*

MISTRESS OVERDONE
What proclamation, man?

What proclamation?

POMPEY
All houses in the suburbs of Vienna must be
plucked down.

*All brothels in the suburbs of Vienna must be
taken down.*

MISTRESS OVERDONE
And what shall become of those in the city?

And what will happen to the ones that are in the city?

POMPEY
They shall stand for seed: they had gone down too,
but that a wise burgher put in for them.

*They will remain: they were about to be torn down too,
But a wise man interceded on their behalf.*

MISTRESS OVERDONE
But shall all our houses of resort in the suburbs be
pulled down?

*But will all of our houses of pleasure in the suburbs be
Torn down?*

POMPEY
To the ground, mistress.

Yes, to the ground, mistress.

MISTRESS OVERDONE
Why, here's a change indeed in the
commonwealth!
What shall become of me?

Well that's a huge change in the
commonwealth!
What will I do?

POMPEY
Come; fear you not: good counsellors lack no
clients: though you change your place, you need
not
change your trade; I'll be your tapster still.
Courage! there will be pity taken on you: you
that
have worn your eyes almost out in the service,
you
will be considered.

Come now; don't be afraid: good counselors
lack no Clients: though you change your place,
you don't need to
Change your trade; I'll still be your tapster.
Have courage! People will take pity on you: you
who
Have worked so very hard for this, you
Will be considered.

MISTRESS OVERDONE
What's to do here, Thomas tapster? let's
withdraw.

What are we doing here, Mister tapster? Let's
leave.

POMPEY
Here comes Signior Claudio, led by the provost
to
prison; and there's Madam Juliet.

Here comes Mister Claudio, led by the provost
to
Prison: and there's Madam Juliet.

Exeunt

Enter Provost, CLAUDIO, JULIET, and
Officers

CLAUDIO
Fellow, why dost thou show me thus to the
world?
Bear me to prison, where I am committed.

Please, why do you shame me like this in front
of the world?
Just take me to prison, where I am committed.

Provost
I do it not in evil disposition,
But from Lord Angelo by special charge.

I'm not doing it to be evil,
It's a special order from Lord Angelo.

CLAUDIO
Thus can the demigod Authority
Make us pay down for our offence by weight
The words of heaven; on whom it will, it will;

And so the demigod Authority
Makes us pay the exact amount of our offence
The words of heaven; whoever it happens to, it

On whom it will not, so; yet still 'tis just.

happens, The same for whoever it doesn't
happen to. Either way, it is justice.

Re-enter LUCIO and two Gentlemen

LUCIO
Why, how now, Claudio! whence comes this
restraint?

Why, what's happened, Claudio! Where do these
chains come from?

CLAUDIO
From too much liberty, my Lucio, liberty:
As surfeit is the father of much fast,
So every scope by the immoderate use
Turns to restraint. Our natures do pursue,
Like rats that ravin down their proper bane,
A thirsty evil; and when we drink we die.

From too much livery, my Lucio, liberty:
Just like someone who fasts then overindulges,
So does every freedom from excessive use
Turn into restrain. Our natures do chase,
Like rats that greedily devour what is poisonous
to them, A thirsty evil; and when we drink, we
die.

LUCIO
If could speak so wisely under an arrest, I would
send for certain of my creditors: and yet, to say
the truth, I had as lief have the foppery of
freedom
as the morality of imprisonment. What's thy
offence, Claudio?

If I could speak with such wisdom while under
arrest, I would Send for certain of the ones who
would imprison me for debt: and yet, to say The
truth, I would rather have the foolishness of
freedom Instead of the morality of
imprisonment. What is your Offence, Claudio?

CLAUDIO
What but to speak of would offend again.

If I speak it, it would be another offence.

LUCIO
What, is't murder?

What, is it murder?

CLAUDIO
No.

LUCIO
Lechery?

CLAUDIO
Call it so.

You could call it that.

Provost
Away, sir! you must go.

Leave, sir! You must go.

CLAUDIO
One word, good friend. Lucio, a word with you.

One word, good friend. Lucio, I want a word
with you.

LUCIO

A hundred, if they'll do you any good.
Is lechery so look'd after?

CLAUDIO
Thus stands it with me: upon a true contract
I got possession of Julietta's bed:
You know the lady; she is fast my wife,
Save that we do the denunciation lack
Of outward order: this we came not to,
Only for propagation of a dower
Remaining in the coffer of her friends,
From whom we thought it meet to hide our love
Till time had made them for us. But it chances
The stealth of our most mutual entertainment
With character too gross is writ on Juliet.

LUCIO
With child, perhaps?

CLAUDIO
Unhappily, even so.
And the new deputy now for the duke—
Whether it be the fault and glimpse of newness,
Or whether that the body public be
A horse whereon the governor doth ride,
Who, newly in the seat, that it may know
He can command, lets it straight feel the spur;
Whether the tyranny be in his place,
Or in his emmence that fills it up,
I stagger in:--but this new governor
Awakes me all the enrolled penalties
Which have, like unscour'd armour, hung by the wall
So long that nineteen zodiacs have gone round
And none of them been worn; and, for a name,
Now puts the drowsy and neglected act
Freshly on me: 'tis surely for a name.

LUCIO
I warrant it is: and thy head stands so tickle on thy shoulders that a milkmaid, if she be in love, may sigh it off. Send after the duke and appeal to
him.

You can have a hundred if they'll do you any good. Is lechery such a punishable crime?

As you see me now: in the presence of witnesses I took to Julietta's bed:
You know her; she is wife bound by pre-contract, Missing only the formal declaration To the public: we didn't make it to that, We were waiting for her dowry That remained in a strongbox with her relatives, From whom we thought it would be best to hide our love Until time had disposed them in our favor. But as our luck would have it The stealth of our mutual love Was undeniably revealed on Juliet's body.

You mean she's with child?

Unfortunately so.
And the new deputy now that has taken place of the duke--- Whether it's a fault from being so new at this Or whether the public body is Merely a horse for him to ride, Who, since he is a new rider, in order to Discipline it and let it know who is in command, at once digs in his spur, Whether the tyranny be inherent in the office, Or in the eminence of him that fills it up, I stagger in:-- but this new governor Awakes all the old penalties Which have, like rusty armor, hung by the wall For so long that nineteen years have gone by And none of them have been worn; and, for the sake of his reputation, Now puts all of the old punishments Freshly on me: surely it is only for a reputation.

*I bet it is: and your head stands so unstable on You shoulders that a milkmaid, if she is in love, could sigh it off. Send a message to the duke and appeal to
him.*

CLAUDIO

I have done so, but he's not to be found.
I prithee, Lucio, do me this kind service:
This day my sister should the cloister enter
And there receive her approbation:
Acquaint her with the danger of my state:
Implore her, in my voice, that she make friends
To the strict deputy; bid herself assay him:
I have great hope in that; for in her youth
There is a prone and speechless dialect,
Such as move men; beside, she hath prosperous art
When she will play with reason and discourse,
And well she can persuade.

LUCIO

I pray she may; as well for the encouragement of the
like, which else would stand under grievous
imposition, as for the enjoying of thy life, who I
would be sorry should be thus foolishly lost at a
game of tick-tack. I'll to her.

CLAUDIO

I thank you, good friend Lucio.

LUCIO

Within two hours.

CLAUDIO

Come, officer, away!

I've done that, but he can't be found.
I ask you, Lucio, do this for me:
Today my sister should enter the monastery
To receive her approbation there:
Tell her about the trouble I'm in:
Ask her, for me, to make friends
With the strict deputy; ask her to attempt to
sway him: I have great hope in that: since she is
so young There is an eager and speechless
language, That moves men; besides that, she has
a skill for gaining favorable results
When she will use reason and rationality,
And she can be very persuasive.

I hope she will; for your sake and for all others
in the same
Situation, which otherwise would suffer serious
Accusation penalties, and would miss out on the
enjoyments of life Which would be a shame to
lose for something as silly As a bed-romp. I'll go
tell her.

I'll be back in two hours.

Come on, officer, let's go!

Exeunt

SCENE III. A monastery.

Enter DUKE VINCENTIO and FRIAR THOMAS

DUKE VINCENTIO
No, holy father; throw away that thought;
Believe not that the dribbling dart of love
Can pierce a complete bosom. Why I desire thee
To give me secret harbour, hath a purpose
More grave and wrinkled than the aims and ends
Of burning youth.

No, holy father, get that thought out of your mind; Don't believe that Cupid's arrow Can pierce a perfect heart. The reason I want you To give me refuge here in secret, has a purpose behind it More serious and mature that the goals and desires Of burning youth.

FRIAR THOMAS
May your grace speak of it?

Will you tell me what it is?

DUKE VINCENTIO
My holy sir, none better knows than you
How I have ever loved the life removed
And held in idle price to haunt assemblies
Where youth, and cost, and witless bravery
keeps.
I have deliver'd to Lord Angelo,
A man of stricture and firm abstinence,
My absolute power and place here in Vienna,
And he supposes me travell'd to Poland;
For so I have strew'd it in the common ear,
And so it is received. Now, pious sir,
You will demand of me why I do this?

My holy sir, no one knows better than you How I have always loved a secluded life And have not thought there was very much worth in going to assemblies Where young and foolish bravado is to be found. I have delivered to Lord Angelo, A very severe and self-restricting man, All of the power and station here in Vienna, And he thinks that I am traveling to Poland; Since that what I have been spreading to the common people, So that's where they think I am. Now, pious sir, You will ask of me why I'm going this?

FRIAR THOMAS
Gladly, my lord.

Gladly, my lord.

DUKE VINCENTIO
We have strict statutes and most biting laws.
The needful bits and curbs to headstrong weeds,
Which for this nineteen years we have let slip;
Even like an o'ergrown lion in a cave,
That goes not out to prey. Now, as fond fathers,
Having bound up the threatening twigs of birch,
Only to stick it in their children's sight
For terror, not to use, in time the rod
Becomes more mock'd than fear'd; so our
decrees,
Dead to infliction, to themselves are dead;
And liberty plucks justice by the nose;

We have strict rules and laws That are necessary for controlling headstrong miscreants, Which we have let slide these last nineteen years; Just like a lion grown fat and inactive in a cave, That doesn't go out to hunt. Now, as foolish fathers, Who bind up twigs for beating their children Only to let them see it and threaten them with For terror, not to actually use it, in time will Become more mocked than feared; that's what has happened To our laws, not being enforced, have become redundant; And freedom contemptuously mocks

The baby beats the nurse, and quite athwart
Goes all decorum.

FRIAR THOMAS
It rested in your grace
To unloose this tied-up justice when you
pleased:
And it in you more dreadful would have seem'd
Than in Lord Angelo.

DUKE VINCENTIO
I do fear, too dreadful:
Sith 'twas my fault to give the people scope,
'Twould be my tyranny to strike and gall them
For what I bid them do: for we bid this be done,
When evil deeds have their permissive pass
And not the punishment. Therefore indeed, my
father,
I have on Angelo imposed the office;
Who may, in the ambush of my name, strike
home,
And yet my nature never in the fight
To do in slander. And to behold his sway,
I will, as 'twere a brother of your order,
Visit both prince and people: therefore, I
prithee,
Supply me with the habit and instruct me
How I may formally in person bear me
Like a true friar. More reasons for this action
At our more leisure shall I render you;
Only, this one: Lord Angelo is precise;
Stands at a guard with envy; scarce confesses
That his blood flows, or that his appetite
Is more to bread than stone: hence shall we see,
If power change purpose, what our seemers be.

*the law; The baby beats the nurse, and propriety
and social order Goes the wrong direction.*

*It was up to you, your grace,
To bring this justice down whenever you chose:
And by doing so, you would have seemed much
more dreadful
Than Lord Angelo.*

*I'm afraid that would have made me too
dreadful: Since it was my fault that I let things
run amuck, I would seem a tyrant to punish and
anger them For what I myself let them get away
with: we virtually order this to be done, When
evil deeds are allowed to pass Without the
punishment. And so, father,
I have imposed that duty onto Angelo;
Who may, under cover of my name, strike home,
And yet my true nature will never have to be put
in the fight
And put in disrepute. And so that I may behold
his effect, I will, disguised as a brother of your
monastery, Visit both the governor and people:
therefore, I as you,
Give me the garb of a priest and instruct me
How it is best to act in front of people
As though I was a real friar. More reasons for
this action I shall tell you when we have more
time; But I will tell you this: Lord Angelo is
extremely strict; He stands with a defensive
posture with malice; Will scarcely Confess that
his blood flows, or that he has And normal
human appetites: so we shall see, If power
changes purpose, what people really are.*

Exeunt

SCENE IV. A nunnery.

Enter ISABELLA and FRANCISCA

ISABELLA
And have you nuns no farther privileges?

Do you have any other rooms?

FRANCISCA
Are not these large enough?

Are these not large enough?

ISABELLA
Yes, truly; I speak not as desiring more;
But rather wishing a more strict restraint
Upon the sisterhood, the votarists of Saint Clare.

They are; I don't mean to speak as if it's not enough; But rather wanting a more strict restraint Upon the sisterhood, the ones who are bound by vows to St. Clare.

LUCIO
[Within] Ho! Peace be in this place!

[Inside] Hello! Is anyone there!

ISABELLA
Who's that which calls?

Who is that calling?

FRANCISCA
It is a man's voice. Gentle Isabella,
Turn you the key, and know his business of him;
You may, I may not; you are yet unsworn.
When you have vow'd, you must not speak with men
But in the presence of the prioress:
Then, if you speak, you must not show your face,
Or, if you show your face, you must not speak.
He calls again; I pray you, answer him.

It's a man's voice. Gentle Isabella, Turn the key and go see what he needs; You can, I am not allowed; you haven't taken your vows yet. When you have sworn, you cannot speak with men Except in the presence of the head of the nunnery: Then, if you speak to a man, you can't show your face, Or, if you show your face, you cannot speak. He just shouted again; please answer him.

Exit

ISABELLA
Peace and prosperity! Who is't that calls

Peace and good health to you! Who is it that is calling?

Enter LUCIO

LUCIO
Hail, virgin, if you be, as those cheek-roses
Proclaim you are no less! Can you so stead me
As bring me to the sight of Isabella,
A novice of this place and the fair sister
To her unhappy brother Claudio?

Hello, virgin, if you are one, as those rosy cheeks Proclaim that you must be! Can you help me By bringing me to see a girl named Isabella, A student of this place and the lovely sister To her unfortunate brother Claudio?

ISABELLA
Why 'her unhappy brother'? let me ask,
The rather for I now must make you know
I am that Isabella and his sister.

Why 'her unfortunate brother'? let me ask Sooner rather than later because, as I now will tell you, I am his sister Isabella who you are looking for.

LUCIO
Gentle and fair, your brother kindly greets you:
Not to be weary with you, he's in prison.

Gentle and beautiful, your brother sends you kind greetings: Not to distress you, but he's in prison.

ISABELLA
Woe me! for what?

Oh no! for what?

LUCIO
For that which, if myself might be his judge,
He should receive his punishment in thanks:
He hath got his friend with child.

The reason is one that if I were his judge I would say his punishment should be gratitude: He has gotten his girl pregnant.

ISABELLA
Sir, make me not your story.

Sir, don't turn me into a joke.

LUCIO
It is true.
I would not--though 'tis my familiar sin
With maids to seem the lapwing and to jest,
Tongue far from heart--play with all virgins so:
I hold you as a thing ensky'd and sainted.
By your renouncement an immortal spirit,
And to be talk'd with in sincerity,
As with a saint.

It's true I would not—though it's often a misdeed a commit With young ladies so I seem like a clever man and to joke around, Tongue in cheek—I wouldn't do this to every maiden: I see you as someone exalted and saintly. Because of your choice to become a nun, you are like an immortal spirit And must be spoken to with sincereity, As one would speak to a saint.

ISABELLA
You do blaspheme the good in mocking me.

You are speaking blasphemy in order to make fun of me.

LUCIO
Do not believe it. Fewness and truth, 'tis thus:
Your brother and his lover have embraced:
As those that feed grow full, as blossoming time
That from the seedness the bare fallow brings
To teeming foison, even so her plenteous womb
Expresseth his full tilth and husbandry.

Don't think that. To be brief and truthful, it's this: Your brother and his lover embraced: As those that grow food, at blossoming time From the seeds planted in the bare earth grow A bountiful harvest, like this her ample womb Shows his work in planting his seed.

ISABELLA
Some one with child by him? My cousin Juliet?

Some one pregnant by him? My cousin Juliet?

LUCIO
Is she your cousin?

Is she your cousin?

ISABELLA

Adoptedly; as school-maids change their names
By vain though apt affection.

By adoption; as school girls may change their names In silliness because of great fondness for each other.

LUCIO

She it is.

It is her.

ISABELLA

O, let him marry her.

Oh, he can marry her.

LUCIO

This is the point.
The duke is very strangely gone from hence;
Bore many gentlemen, myself being one,
In hand and hope of action: but we do learn
By those that know the very nerves of state,
His givings-out were of an infinite distance
From his true-meant design. Upon his place,
And with full line of his authority,
Governs Lord Angelo; a man whose blood
Is very snow-broth; one who never feels
The wanton stings and motions of the sense,
But doth rebate and blunt his natural edge
With profits of the mind, study and fast.
He--to give fear to use and liberty,
Which have for long run by the hideous law,
As mice by lions--hath pick'd out an act,
Under whose heavy sense your brother's life
Falls into forfeit: he arrests him on it;
And follows close the rigour of the statute,
To make him an example. All hope is gone,
Unless you have the grace by your fair prayer
To soften Angelo: and that's my pith of business
'Twixt you and your poor brother.

*That is the point.
The duke is very strangely absent from here;
Misled many men, including myself,
Waiting in hope for military action: but we did learn From those that know important people in government That his words were very far From his real intentions. Instead of him, And with all of his authority, Lord Angelo is govenor; a man whose blood Is cold like melted snow; one who never feels The unrestrained itching and urges of the senses But instead suppresses and blunts his natural desire With improving his mind, studying and fasting. He—to put fear into our customs and freedoms, Which have long by-passed the frightening law, As mice run by lions—has picked out a crime, Whose grave sentence is that your brother's life Is to be given as punishment: he arrests him because of it; And closely follows the rigorous laws, In order to make him an example. All hope is gone, Unless you have the good fortune from your prayers Needed to soften Angelo: and that is the reason of problem Between you and your poor brother*

ISABELLA

Doth he so seek his life?

Does he beg for his life?

LUCIO

Has censured him
Already; and, as I hear, the provost hath
A warrant for his execution.

*He is condemned
Already; and, as I hear, the provost has
A warrant for his execution.*

ISABELLA

Alas! what poor ability's in me

Oh no! what power do I have

To do him good?

LUCIO
Assay the power you have.

ISABELLA
My power? Alas, I doubt--

LUCIO
Our doubts are traitors
And make us lose the good we oft might win
By fearing to attempt. Go to Lord Angelo,
And let him learn to know, when maidens sue,
Men give like gods; but when they weep and kneel,
All their petitions are as freely theirs
As they themselves would owe them.

ISABELLA
I'll see what I can do.

LUCIO
But speedily.

ISABELLA
I will about it straight;
No longer staying but to give the mother
Notice of my affair. I humbly thank you:
Commend me to my brother: soon at night
I'll send him certain word of my success.

LUCIO
I take my leave of you.

ISABELLA
Good sir, adieu.

to do him any good?

Try what power you do have.

My power? But, I don't know--

*We do harm by doubting ourselves
And lose the benefits we often might win
Because we are afraid to try. Go to Lord
Angelo, And let him learn that when maidens
plead, Men give in like gods; but when they
weep and kneel,
All their requests are granted exactly
As they wanted them to be.*

I'll see what I can do.

But do it quickly.

*I will do it immediately;
Not staying any longer than to give the head of
the nunnery Notice of my business. I humbly
thank you: Pass my good wishes onto my
brother: early this evening I'll send him news of
the result of my attempts.*

I bid you good bye.

Good sir, farewell.

Exeunt

ACT II

SCENE I. A hall In ANGELO's house.

ANGELO

We must not make a scarecrow of the law,
Setting it up to fear the birds of prey,
And let it keep one shape, till custom make it
Their perch and not their terror.

We cannot make the law into a scarecorw,
Set up to frighten the birds of prey,
And let it do only this one thing, until this
routine turns it into Their habitat and not
something they fear.

ESCALUS

Ay, but yet
Let us be keen, and rather cut a little,
Than fall, and bruise to death. Alas, this
gentleman
Whom I would save, had a most noble father!
Let but your honour know,
Whom I believe to be most strait in virtue,
That, in the working of your own affections,
Had time cohered with place or place with
wishing,
Or that the resolute acting of your blood
Could have attain'd the effect of your own
purpose,
Whether you had not sometime in your life
Err'd in this point which now you censure him,
And pull'd the law upon you.

Yes, but still
Let us be careful, and rather change a little at a
time, Than let it fall heavily and get bashed to
death. Sadly, this gentleman
Whom I would save, had a most noble father!
Only let your honorableness consider,
Which I believe to be very proper in virtue,
That, in the functioning of your own desires,
Had a point in time come together with a place,
or a place with a desire,
Or with the purposeful action of your own
passion You could have achieved the object of
your desire,
Would you not, at some point in your life,
Make the mistake for which you now punish
him, And have brought the law down on
yourself.

ANGELO

'Tis one thing to be tempted, Escalus,
Another thing to fall. I not deny
The jury, passing on the prisoner's life,
May in the sworn twelve have a thief or two
Guiltier than him they try. What's open made to
justice,
That justice seizes: what know the laws
That thieves do pass on thieves? 'Tis very
pregnant,
The jewel that we find, we stoop and take't
Because we see it; but what we do not see
We tread upon, and never think of it.
You may not so extenuate his offence
For I have had such faults; but rather tell me,
When I, that censure him, do so offend,
Let mine own judgment pattern out my death,

It is one thing to be tempted, Escalus,
And another thing to give in to the temptation. I
do not deny That the jury, which passes
judgement on the prisoner's life, May have thief
or two in the twelve that are sworn in That are
more guilty than those they try. It is what is
made known to the law, That the law tries: what
knowledge can the laws take About the
possibility that thieves may pass sentence on
other thieves? It is clear that When we find a
gem, we stoop and take it Because we see it: but
what we do not see We walk over, and never
think of it. You may not make allowances for his
offence Because I have had similar mistakes;
but instead tell me When I, that punish him,
make the same mistake, Let my own sentence

And nothing come in partial. Sir, he must die.

ESCALUS
Be it as your wisdom will.

ANGELO
Where is the provost?

PROVOST
Here, if it like your honour.

ANGELO
See that Claudio
Be executed by nine to-morrow morning:
Bring him his confessor, let him be prepared;
For that's the utmost of his pilgrimage.

ESCALUS
[Aside] Well, heaven forgive him! and forgive
us all!
Some rise by sin, and some by virtue fall:
Some run from brakes of ice, and answer none:
And some condemned for a fault alone.

ELBOW
Come, bring them away: if these be good people
in
a commonweal that do nothing but use their
abuses in
common houses, I know no law: bring them
away.

ANGELO
How now, sir! What's your name? and what's
the matter?

ELBOW
If it Please your honour, I am the poor duke's
constable, and my name is Elbow: I do lean
upon
justice, sir, and do bring in here before your
good

serve as a model for my death, And let there be
no mitigation. Sir, he must die.

Be it as your wisdom wills it.

Where is the provost?

I am here if it is pleases you, your honor.

See to it that Claudio
Be executed by nine in the morning tomorrow:
Bring him his confessor, so he can be prepared,
For the last point in his journey.

Exit Provost

[Aside] Well, God forgive him! and forgive all
of us!
Some rise up by sin, and some fall from virtue:
Some commit sin and escape the consequences:
And some are condemned for only a mistake.

Enter ELBOW, and Officers with FROTH and
POMPEY

Come, take them away: if these be good people
in
A community that do nothing but practice their
vices in
Brothels, I do not know the law: take them
away.

What is the meaning of this, sir! What's your
name? and what's the matter?

It it pleases you, your hono, I am the Duke's
poor Constable, and my name is Elbow: I do
rely on
justice, sir, and do bring in here before your
good

honour two notorious benefactors.

Honor two notorious benefactors.

ANGELO
Benefactors? Well; what benefactors are they? Are
they not malefactors?

Benefactors? Well; what kind of benefactors are they? Are
They not malefactors?

ELBOW
If it? please your honour, I know not well what they
are: but precise villains they are, that I am sure
of; and void of all profanation in the world that
good Christians ought to have.

If it pleases you, your honor, I do not know well what they
Are: but they are definitely villains, that I am sure of; and devoid of all 'profanation' in the world that Good Christians should have.

ESCALUS
This comes off well; here's a wise officer.

This is well spoken; here's a wise officer.

ANGELO
Go to: what quality are they of? Elbow is your
name? why dost thou not speak, Elbow?

Go on: what occupation are they? Elbow is your Name? What are you not speaking, Elbow?

POMPEY
He cannot, sir; he's out at elbow.

He cannot, sir; he's a bit dumb, and doesn't always make sense.

ANGELO
What are you, sir?

What are you, sir?

ELBOW
He, sir! a tapster, sir; parcel-bawd; one that
serves a bad woman; whose house, sir, was, as they
say, plucked down in the suburbs; and now she
professes a hot-house, which, I think, is a very
ill house too.

Sir, He is a bar man, sir; a part-time procurer of whores; one that Works for a bad woman; whose brothel, sir, was, as they Say, torn down in the suburbs; and now she Claims to run a bath-house, which I think, is a very bad house too.

ESCALUS
How know you that?

How do you know that?

ELBOW
My wife, sir, whom I detest before heaven and
your honour,--

My wife, sir, whom I 'detest' before heaven and your honor,--

ESCALUS
How? thy wife?

Your wife? Why?

ELBOW

Ay, sir; whom, I thank heaven, is an honest
woman,--

ESCALUS
Dost thou detest her therefore?

ELBOW
I say, sir, I will detest myself also, as well as
she, that this house, if it be not a bawd's house,
it is pity of her life, for it is a naughty house.

ESCALUS
How dost thou know that, constable?

ELBOW
Marry, sir, by my wife; who, if she had been a
woman
cardinally given, might have been accused in
fornication, adultery, and all uncleanliness there.

ESCALUS
By the woman's means?

ELBOW
Ay, sir, by Mistress Overdone's means: but as
she
spit in his face, so she defied him.

POMPEY
Sir, if it please your honour, this is not so.

ELBOW
Prove it before these varlets here, thou
honourable
man; prove it.

ESCALUS
Do you hear how he misplaces?

POMPEY
Sir, she came in great with child; and longing,
saving your honour's reverence, for stewed
prunes;
sir, we had but two in the house, which at that
very

---

*Yes, sir; whom, I thank heaven, is an honest
woman,--*

Why do you detest her then?

*I say, sir, I will 'detest' myself—I mean declare
myself—also, along with Her, that this house, if
it isn't a brothel, It is sad thing for her, for it as
a wicked house.*

How do you know this, constable?

*I swear by the Virgin Mary, sir, and by my wife;
who if she had been a woman
That was carnally inclined, might have been
accused of Fornication, adultery, and all moral
impuity there.*

By this woman's doings?

*Yes, sir, by Mistress Overdone's doings: but the
same as she
Spit in Pompey's face, so she defied him.*

Sir, if it pleases you, your honor, this is not true.

*Prove it before these 'scoundrels' here then, you
'honorable
Man'; prove it.*

*Do you hear how me mistakes one word for
another?*

*Sir, she came in pregnant; and wanting--
Begging your pardon for my bad language—for
stewed prunes;
Sir, we had only two in the house, which at that
very*

distant time stood, as it were, in a fruit-dish, a
dish of some three-pence; your honours have
seen
such dishes; they are not China dishes, but very
good dishes,--

ESCALUS
Go to, go to: no matter for the dish, sir.

POMPEY
No, indeed, sir, not of a pin; you are therein in
the right: but to the point. As I say, this
Mistress Elbow, being, as I say, with child, and
being great-bellied, and longing, as I said, for
prunes; and having but two in the dish, as I said,
Master Froth here, this very man, having eaten
the
rest, as I said, and, as I say, paying for them
very
honestly; for, as you know, Master Froth, I
could
not give you three-pence again.

FROTH
No, indeed.

POMPEY
Very well: you being then, if you be
remembered,
cracking the stones of the foresaid prunes,--

FROTH
Ay, so I did indeed.

POMPEY
Why, very well; I telling you then, if you be
remembered, that such a one and such a one
were past
cure of the thing you wot of, unless they kept
very
good diet, as I told you,--

FROTH
All this is true.

POMPEY

*Instant of time stood, as it were, in a fruit-dish,
a Dish worth about three pennies; your honors
have seen
Dishes like that; they aren't China dishes, but
very Good dihes,--*

Go on, go on: no matter about the dish, sir.

*No, indeed, sir, it's not worth the trifle; you are
thus Correct: but to the point. As I say, this
Mistress Elbow, being, as I say, with child, and
Being great-eblied, and wanting, as I said, for
Prunes; and having only two in the dish, as I
said, Master Froth here, this man here, having
eaten the
Others, as I said, and, as I say, he payed for
them
Honestly; for, as you know, Master Frother, I
can't
Give you three pennies again.*

No, indeed.

*Very well: you were then, if you remember,
Cracking the stones of the aforementioned
prunes,--*

Yes, I did do that.

*Why, yes; I told you then, if you
Remember, that so-and-so and so-and-so were
beyond
Cure for that thing you know of, syphilis, unless
they kept a very
Good diet, as I told you,--*

All this is true.

Why, very well, then,--

ESCALUS
Come, you are a tedious fool: to the purpose. What
was done to Elbow's wife, that he hath cause to
complain of? Come me to what was done to her.

POMPEY
Sir, your honour cannot come to that yet.

ESCALUS
No, sir, nor I mean it not.

POMPEY
Sir, but you shall come to it, by your honour's
leave. And, I beseech you, look into Master
Froth
here, sir; a man of four-score pound a year;
whose
father died at Hallowmas: was't not at
Hallowmas,
Master Froth?

FROTH
All-hallond eve.

POMPEY
Why, very well; I hope here be truths. He, sir,
sitting, as I say, in a lower chair, sir; 'twas in
the Bunch of Grapes, where indeed you have a
delight
to sit, have you not?

FROTH
I have so; because it is an open room and good
for winter.

POMPEY
Why, very well, then; I hope here be truths.

ANGELO
This will last out a night in Russia,
When nights are longest there: I'll take my
leave.

Why, very well, then,--

*Come one, you are a tedious fool: get to the
point. What
Was done to Elbow's wide, that he has a reason
to Complain? Come the part about what was
done to her.*

Sir, your honor cannot come to that yet.

No, sir, I don't mean it that way.

*Sir, but you shall come to it, by your honor's
Leave. And, I ask you, consider Master Froth
Here, sir; a man of 80 pounds a year, a good
income; whose
Father died on All Saint's Day: was it not on All
Saint's Day,
Master Froth?*

Halloween.

*Why, very well; I hope all this is true. He, sir,
Was sitting, as I say, in a low chair, sir; 'it was
in The room called Bunch of Grapes, where
indeed you like
To sit, do you not?*

*I do like it; because it is an public room and
good for winter.*

Why, very well, ten; I hope this is the truth.

*This will take a very long time, like Russian
nights, As nights are the longest there: I'll take
my leave.*

And leave you to the hearing of the cause;
Hoping you'll find good cause to whip them all.

ESCALUS
I think no less. Good morrow to your lordship.

Now, sir, come on: what was done to Elbow's wife, once more?

POMPEY
Once, sir? there was nothing done to her once.

ELBOW
I beseech you, sir, ask him what this man did to my wife.

POMPEY
I beseech your honour, ask me.

ESCALUS
Well, sir; what did this gentleman to her?

POMPEY
I beseech you, sir, look in this gentleman's face. Good Master Froth, look upon his honour; 'tis for a
good purpose. Doth your honour mark his face?

ESCALUS
Ay, sir, very well.

POMPEY
Nay; I beseech you, mark it well.

ESCALUS
Well, I do so.

POMPEY
Doth your honour see any harm in his face?

ESCALUS
Why, no.

POMPEY

*And leave you to the hearing of the case;
I hope you'll find a good reason to whip them all.*

I think the same. Good night to you lordship.

Exit ANGELO

Now, sir, come on: Once more, what was done to Elbow's wife?

Once, sir? There was nothing done to her once.

I implore you, sir, ask him what this man did to my wife/

I implore your honor, ask me.

Well, sir; what did this gentleman do to her?

I implore you, sir, look in this gentleman's face Good Master Froth, look at his honor, it is for a Good reason. Does your honor take note of his face?

Yes, sir, very well.

No, I implore you, not it well.

Well, I do so.

Does your honor see any malice in his face?

Why, no.

I'll be supposed upon a book, his face is the worst
thing about him. Good, then; if his face be the worst thing about him, how could Master Froth do the
constable's wife any harm? I would know that of your honour.

*I'll swear on the Bible, the rest of him is as harmless
As his face. Good, then; if the rest of him is
As harmless as his face, how could Master Frother do the Constable's wife any harm? I would know if that has happened
Your honor.*

ESCALUS
He's in the right. Constable, what say you to it?

He's right. Constable, what do you have to say about it?

ELBOW
First, an it like you, the house is a respected house; next, this is a respected fellow; and his mistress is a respected woman.

First, if it please you, the house is a 'respected' House; next, this is a 'respected' fellow; and his Mistress is a 'respected' woman.

POMPEY
By this hand, sir, his wife is a more respected person than any of us all.

By these facts, sir, his wife is the most 'respected' Person of us all. [Aside] That fool Elbow thinks we mean suspected of sexual dealings.

ELBOW
Varlet, thou liest; thou liest, wicked varlet! The time has yet to come that she was ever respected with man, woman, or child.

Scoundrel, you lie; you like, horrible scoundrel! The Time hasn't yet come that she was ever 'respected' To be with any man, woman, or child.

POMPEY
Sir, she was respected with him before he married with her.

Sir, she was 'respected' with him before he married her.

ESCALUS
Which is the wiser here? Justice or Iniquity? Is this true?

Which is true here? The character of Justice or Injustice? Is This true?

ELBOW
O thou caitiff! O thou varlet! O thou wicked Hannibal! I respected with her before I was married
to her! If ever I was respected with her, or she with me, let not your worship think me the poor duke's officer. Prove this, thou wicked Hannibal, or
I'll have mine action of battery on thee.

*Oh you villain! Oh you scoundrel! Oh you wicked Hannibal—I mean cannibal! To think I 'respected' with her before I was married
To her! If ever I was 'resepcted' with her, or she With me, then your honor don't think that I am the Duke's poor constable. Prove this, you terrible Hannibal, or
I'll my lawsuit for assault on you.*

ESCALUS

If he took you a box o' the ear, you might have your
action of slander too.

If he hit you, you might have your
Lawsuit for slander too. Hah, again, he
confused his words.

ELBOW
Marry, I thank your good worship for it. What is't
your worship's pleasure I shall do with this wicked caitiff?

I swear on the Virgin Mary, I thank you good
honor for that. What do
You want, you honor, for me to do with this
wicked villain?

ESCALUS
Truly, officer, because he hath some offences in him
that thou wouldst discover if thou couldst, let him
continue in his courses till thou knowest what they
are.

It is true, officer, since he has committed some
offences
That you would reveal if you could, let him
Continue in his way of life till you know what
the offences
Are.

ELBOW
Marry, I thank your worship for it. Thou seest, thou
wicked varlet, now, what's come upon thee: thou art
to continue now, thou varlet; thou art to continue.

By the Virgin Mary, I thank your honor for this.
You see, you
Wicked scoundrel, now, what is about to happen
to you: you are
To continue now, you scoundrel: you are to
continue.

ESCALUS
Where were you born, friend?

Where were you born, friend?

FROTH
Here in Vienna, sir.

Here in Vienna, sir.

ESCALUS
Are you of fourscore pounds a year?

Do you make 80 pounds a year?

FROTH
Yes, an't please you, sir.

Yes, if it pleases you, sir.

ESCALUS
So. What trade are you of, sir?

So. What is your occupation, sor?

POMPHEY
Tapster; a poor widow's tapster.

A bar man; a poor widow's bar man.

ESCALUS

Your mistress' name?

POMPHEY
Mistress Overdone.

ESCALUS
Hath she had any more than one husband?

POMPEY
Nine, sir; Overdone by the last.

ESCALUS
Nine! Come hither to me, Master Froth. Master
Froth, I would not have you acquainted with
tapsters: they will draw you, Master Froth, and
you
will hang them. Get you gone, and let me hear
no
more of you.

FROTH
I thank your worship. For mine own part, I
never
come into any room in a tap-house, but I am
drawn
in.

ESCALUS
Well, no more of it, Master Froth: farewell.

Come you hither to me, Master tapster. What's
your
name, Master tapster?

POMPEY
Pompey.

ESCALUS
What else?

POMPEY
Bum, sir.

What is your mistress' name?

Mistress Overdone.

Did she have more than one husband?

*Nine, sir; She got the name Overdone from the
last.*

*Nine! Come to me, Master Froth. Master
Froth, I would not have thought to acquaint you
with Bar men: they will cheat you, Master
Froth, and you
Be the reason they are hung. Get away from
here, and don't let me hear any
More from you.*

*I thank you, your honor. For my own part, I
never
Go into any room in a tavern, unless I am lead
In.*

Well, no matter, Master Froth: farewell.

Exit FROTH

*Come to me, Master bar man, What is your
Name, Master bar man?*

Pompey.

What else?

ESCALUS

Troth, and your bum is the greatest thing about you;
so that in the beastliest sense you are Pompey the
Great. Pompey, you are partly a bawd, Pompey,
howsoever you colour it in being a tapster, are you
not? come, tell me true: it shall be the better for you.

Truth, and your bum is the greatest, and crudest, thing about you;
So that in the lowest sense you are Pompey the Great. Pompey, you are partly a whore procurer, Pompey,
However you hide it by being a bar man, don't You? Come on, tell me the truth: it shall be better for you.

POMPEY

Truly, sir, I am a poor fellow that would live.

Truly, sir, I am a poor fellow that wants to earn a living.

ESCALUS

How would you live, Pompey? by being a bawd? What
do you think of the trade, Pompey? is it a lawful trade?

How do you want to earn a living, Pompey? By procuring whores? What
Do you think of that occupation, Pompey? Is it a lawful occupation?

POMPEY

If the law would allow it, sir.

If only it was allowed by the law, sir.

ESCALUS

But the law will not allow it, Pompey; nor it shall
not be allowed in Vienna.

But it is not allowed by the law, Pompey; and it will
Not be allowed in Vienna.

POMPEY

Does your worship mean to geld and splay all the
youth of the city?

Does you honor mean to neuter and spay all the Young men and women in the city?

ESCALUS

No, Pompey.

No, Pompey.

POMPEY

Truly, sir, in my poor opinion, they will to't then.
If your worship will take order for the drabs and
the knaves, you need not to fear the bawds.

Truly then, sir, in my low opinion, they will continue then.
If your honor would take care of the whores and Their clients, you wouldn't need to worry about the procurers.

ESCALUS

There are pretty orders beginning, I can tell you:
it is but heading and hanging.

There are considerable laws starting now, I can tell you: The punishment will only be beheading and hanging.

POMPEY

If you head and hang all that offend that way but for ten year together, you'll be glad to give out a commission for more heads: if this law hold in Vienna ten year, I'll rent the fairest house in it after three-pence a bay: if you live to see this come to pass, say Pompey told you so.

If you behead and hang all those that commit this offense For only ten years, you'll have to give out an Order for more people: if this law remains in Vienna for ten years, I'll rent the nicest house in it At the rate of three-pennies a room: if you live to see this Happen, say Pompey told you so.

ESCALUS
Thank you, good Pompey; and, in requital of your
prophecy, hark you: I advise you, let me not find you before me again upon any complaint whatsoever;
no, not for dwelling where you do: if I do, Pompey,
I shall beat you to your tent, and prove a shrewd Caesar to you; in plain dealing, Pompey, I shall have you whipt: so, for this time, Pompey, fare you well.

Thank you, good Pompey! and in repayment for your
Prophecy, listen: I advise, you, don't let me find You in front of me again for any complaint whatsoever;
Not, not for living where you do: if I do, Pompey,
I shall beat you to your home, and prove to be a mean Caesar to your Pompey, as Caesar defeated Pompey the Great in battle; to put it plainly, Pompey, I will Have you whipped: so, for now, Pompey, fare you well.

POMPEY
I thank your worship for your good counsel:

I thank your honor for you good advice:

Aside

but I shall follow it as the flesh and fortune shall better determine.
Whip me? No, no; let carman whip his jade:
The valiant heart is not whipt out of his trade.

but I will follow it as my body and opportinuty will Dictate.
Whip me? No, no let a cart driver whip his nag: The courageous heart is not whipped out of his occupation.

Exit

ESCALUS
Come hither to me, Master Elbow; come hither, Master
constable. How long have you been in this place of constable?

Come to me, Master Elbow; come here, Master Constable. How long have you been in this position of constable?

ELBOW
Seven year and a half, sir.

Seven and a half years, sir.

ESCALUS
I thought, by your readiness in the office, you had
continued in it some time. You say, seven years

I thought, by your eagerness in your work, that you had
Held the position for some time. You say, seven

together?

ELBOW
And a half, sir.

ESCALUS
Alas, it hath been great pains to you. They do you
wrong to put you so oft upon 't: are there not men
in your ward sufficient to serve it?

ELBOW
Faith, sir, few of any wit in such matters: as they
are chosen, they are glad to choose me for them; I
do it for some piece of money, and go through with
all.

ESCALUS
Look you bring me in the names of some six or seven,
the most sufficient of your parish.

ELBOW
To your worship's house, sir?

ESCALUS
To my house. Fare you well.

What's o'clock, think you?

JUSTICE
Eleven, sir.

ESCALUS
I pray you home to dinner with me.

JUSTICE
I humbly thank you.

ESCALUS
It grieves me for the death of Claudio;

---

years all together?

And a half, sir.

*Sadly, it's been great trouble for you. They do you
Wrong to put you to work for so long: are there not men
In your district competent enough to work?*

*By heaven, sir, few with any intelligence of these
matters: as they Are chosen, they are glad for
me to take their place; I
Do it in exchange for a bit of money, and go
through with
Everything.*

*Well, bring me the names of about six or seven others,
The most competent in your district.*

To your honor's house, sir?

To my house. Farewell.

Exit ELBOW

What time do you think it is?

Eleven, sir.

I invite you home for dinner with me.

Humbly, I thank you.

It pains me that we will execute Claudio;

But there's no remedy.

But there's nothing to be done.

JUSTICE
Lord Angelo is severe.

Lord Angelo is harsh.

ESCALUS
It is but needful:
Mercy is not itself, that oft looks so;
Pardon is still the nurse of second woe:
But yet,--poor Claudio! There is no remedy.
Come, sir.

It's still necessary:
What looks like mercy isn't always;
Since pardoning may actually encourage a
second offence: But still,--poor Claudio! There
is nothing to be done Come on, sir.

Exeunt

SCENE II. Another room in the same.

SERVANT
He's hearing of a cause; he will come straight
I'll tell him of you.

*He's listening to a case; he will come right out
I'll tell him you're here.*

PROVOST
Pray you, do.

Please do.

Exit SERVANT

I'll know
His pleasure; may be he will relent. Alas,
He hath but as offended in a dream!
All sects, all ages smack of this vice; and he
To die for't!

*I'll know
His intention; perhaps he will change his mind.
Sadly, Claudio has only done wrong like he was
in a dream! All types of people, of all ages have
committed this offence; and he Is to die for it!*

Enter ANGELO

ANGELO
Now, what's the matter. Provost?

Now, what's the wrong, Provost?

PROVOST
Is it your will Claudio shall die tomorrow?

Do you want Claudio to die tomorrow?

ANGELO
Did not I tell thee yea? hadst thou not order?
Why dost thou ask again?

*Didn't I already tell you yes? Don'y you have
the order? Why do you ask again?*

PROVOST
Lest I might be too rash:
Under your good correction, I have seen,
When, after execution, judgment hath
Repented o'er his doom.

*In case I might be too hasty:
Correct me if I'm wrong, but I have seen
When, after an execution, a judge has
Regretted the sentence he gave.*

ANGELO
Go to; let that be mine:
Do you your office, or give up your place,
And you shall well be spared.

*Go on; let that be my worry:
Do your job, or give it up,
And we will manage just as well without you.*

PROVOST
I crave your honour's pardon.
What shall be done, sir, with the groaning
Juliet?

*I'm very sorry, your honor.
What shall be done with Juliet, sir? She is labor
And very near to giving birth.*

She's very near her hour.

ANGELO
Dispose of her
To some more fitter place, and that with speed.

Make arrangments for her
To go to a more fit place for giving birth, and so
quickly.

Re-enter SERVANT

SERVANT
Here is the sister of the man condemn'd
Desires access to you.

Here is the sister of the condemned man
She wishes to speak to you.

ANGELO
Hath he a sister?

He has a sister?

PROVOST
Ay, my good lord; a very virtuous maid,
And to be shortly of a sisterhood,
If not already.

Yes, my good lord; a very virtuous young lady,
And about to become a nun
If she isn't one already.

ANGELO
Well, let her be admitted.

Well, let her come in.

Exit SERVANT

See you the fornicatress be removed:
Let have needful, but not lavish, means;
There shall be order for't.

See you have the pregnant woman moved:
Let her have what she needs, but nothing fancy;
There will be authorization for it.

Enter ISABELLA and LUCIO

PROVOST
God save your honour!

Be well, your honor!

ANGELO
Stay a little while.

Stay a little while.

To ISABELLA

You're welcome: what's your will?

Welcome: what can I do for you?

ISABELLA
I am a woeful suitor to your honour,
Please but your honour hear me.

I wish I was not a petitioner to you, your honor,
But please listen to what I have to say, your
honor.

ANGELO

44

Well; what's your suit?

Well: what are you here for?

ISABELLA
There is a vice that most I do abhor,
And most desire should meet the blow of
justice;
For which I would not plead, but that I must;
For which I must not plead, but that I am
At war 'twixt will and will not.

There is an offence that I do hate,
And very much wish that it should be punished;
For which I would not ask otherwise, except that
I have to;
For which I cannot ask, but that I am
Torn between wanting to and not wanting to.

ANGELO
Well; the matter?

Well; what's the reason?

ISABELLA
I have a brother is condemn'd to die:
I do beseech you, let it be his fault,
And not my brother.

My brother is condemned to die:
I implore you, let the offence be condemned,
Instead of my brother.

PROVOST
[Aside] Heaven give thee moving graces!

[Aside] God grant you persuasiveness!

ANGELO
Condemn the fault and not the actor of it?
Why, every fault's condemn'd ere it be done:
Mine were the very cipher of a function,
To fine the faults whose fine stands in record,
And let go by the actor.

Condemn the offence and not the offender?
Why, every offence is already condemned by it's
nature: My role as judge is meaningless,
I punish the offences whose punishments are set
down in the law And let the offender go
unpunished.

ISABELLA
O just but severe law!
I had a brother, then. Heaven keep your honour!

Oh law, you are right but harsh!
I will no longer have a brother, then. May
Heaven keep you, your honor!

LUCIO
[Aside to ISABELLA] Give't not o'er so: to him
again, entreat him;
Kneel down before him, hang upon his gown:
You are too cold; if you should need a pin,
You could not with more tame a tongue desire
it:
To him, I say!

[Aside to ISABELLA] Don't give up so easily:
go to him again, and plead with him;
Kneel down before him, pull at his gown:
You are too detached; if you need something,
You couldn't ask for it in a more plan way:
Go to him, I say!

ISABELLA
Must he needs die?

Does he have to die?

ANGELO
Maiden, no remedy.

Miss, there is no other way.

ISABELLA

Yes; I do think that you might pardon him,
And neither heaven nor man grieve at the mercy.

Yes, I think you could pardon him,
And neither heaven nor man look down on such mercy.

ANGELO

I will not do't.

I will not do it.

ISABELLA

But can you, if you would?

But could you, if you wanted to?

ANGELO

Look, what I will not, that I cannot do.

Look, I cannot do it if I don't want to do it.

ISABELLA

But might you do't, and do the world no wrong,
If so your heart were touch'd with that remorse
A s mine is to him?

But you could do it, and do the world no wrong
If your heart was touched with compassion
As mine is for him?

ANGELO

He's sentenced; 'tis too late.

He's sentenced: it is too late.

LUCIO

[Aside to ISABELLA] You are too cold.

[Aside to ISABELLA] You are too detached.

ISABELLA

Too late? why, no; I, that do speak a word
May call it back again. Well, believe this,
No ceremony that to great ones 'longs,
Not the king's crown, nor the deputed sword,
The marshal's truncheon, nor the judge's robe,
Become them with one half so good a grace
As mercy does.
If he had been as you and you as he,
You would have slipt like him; but he, like you,
Would not have been so stern.

Too late? Why no; I, if I speak a word
May take it back again. Well, believe this,
No ceremony that belongs to great ones,
Not the king's crown, nor the sword of justice
The military officer's command staff, nor the
judge's robe Suits them half as virtuously
As mercy does.
If he had been in your position and you in his,
You would have slipped up like him; but he, as
you are, Would not have been so stern.

ANGELO

Pray you, be gone.

Please leave.

ISABELLA

I would to heaven I had your potency,
And you were Isabel! should it then be thus?
No; I would tell what 'twere to be a judge,
And what a prisoner.

I wish to God I had your power,
And you were Isabel! Should it be then the way
it is? No; I would show what it meant to be a
judge, And what a prisoner.

LUCIO
[Aside to ISABELLA]
Ay, touch him; there's the vein.

Yes, touch him; that's the way to go about it.

ANGELO
Your brother is a forfeit of the law,
And you but waste your words.

Your brother is subject to the law,
And you are only wasting your words.

ISABELLA
Alas, alas!
Why, all the souls that were were forfeit once;
And He that might the vantage best have took
Found out the remedy. How would you be,
If He, which is the top of judgment, should
But judge you as you are? O, think on that;
And mercy then will breathe within your lips,
Like man new made.

Dear me!
Why, all the souls that ever existed were given
up before the arrival of Christ, And God, who
had the best opportunity to comdemn them,
Found a better way. How would you be,
If God, who is the final judge, should
Judge you as you are? Oh, think about that;
And you will find your mercy,
Like man after salvation.

ANGELO
Be you content, fair maid;
It is the law, not I condemn your brother:
Were he my kinsman, brother, or my son,
It should be thus with him: he must die
tomorrow.

Calm down, young lady
It is the law that sentences your brother, not me.
Even if her were a member of my family, my
brother, or my son, It would still be the same for
him: he will die tomorrow.

ISABELLA
To-morrow! O, that's sudden! Spare him, spare
him!
He's not prepared for death. Even for our
kitchens
We kill the fowl of season: shall we serve
heaven
With less respect than we do minister
To our gross selves? Good, good my lord,
bethink you;
Who is it that hath died for this offence?
There's many have committed it.

Tomorrow! Oh, that's so soon! Spare him, spare
him!
He's not ready to die. Even in the kitchen
One kills the birds when they are ready: shall
we serve heaven
With less respect than we attend
To our mortal selves? My very good lord, please
consider;
Who is it that dies for this offence?
There are many people who have committed it.

LUCIO
[Aside to ISABELLA] Ay, well said.

[Aside to ISABELLA] Yes, well said.

ANGELO
The law hath not been dead, though it hath slept:
Those many had not dared to do that evil,
If the first that did the edict infringe
Had answer'd for his deed: now 'tis awake,

The law hasn't been dead, though it has been
inactive: The many who broke this law would
not have dared to, If the first one who did break
the law Had been punished for it: now the law is

Takes note of what is done; and, like a prophet,
Looks in a glass, that shows what future evils,
Either new, or by remissness new-conceived,
And so in progress to be hatch'd and born,
Are now to have no successive degrees,
But, ere they live, to end.

ISABELLA
Yet show some pity.

ANGELO
I show it most of all when I show justice;
For then I pity those I do not know,
Which a dismiss'd offence would after gall;
And do him right that, answering one foul wrong,
Lives not to act another. Be satisfied;
Your brother dies to-morrow; be content.

ISABELLA
So you must be the first that gives this sentence,
And he, that suffer's. O, it is excellent
To have a giant's strength; but it is tyrannous
To use it like a giant.

LUCIO
[Aside to ISABELLA] That's well said.

ISABELLA
Could great men thunder
As Jove himself does, Jove would ne'er be quiet,
For every pelting, petty officer
Would use his heaven for thunder;
Nothing but thunder! Merciful Heaven,
Thou rather with thy sharp and sulphurous bolt
Split'st the unwedgeable and gnarled oak
Than the soft myrtle: but man, proud man,
Drest in a little brief authority,
Most ignorant of what he's most assured,
His glassy essence, like an angry ape,
Plays such fantastic tricks before high heaven
As make the angels weep; who, with our spleens,
Would all themselves laugh mortal.

---

*in action, It looks at what has been done; and,
like a prophet, Looks in a crystal ball, that
shows what future troubles, Either new, or
brought about by moral impurity only just
thought of, And therefore in progress to being
planned and carried out, Are to have no further
progress, And instead, before they live, are put
to death.*

Yet show some pity.

*I show pity most of all when I uphold the law;
For then I pity those I do not know,
Who would be upset afterwards by an
overlooked offence; And do him right because,
by responding to one bad deed,
He doesn't live to commit another. Be satisfied;
Your brother dies tomorrow; be content.*

*So you will be the frist to give this sentence,
And he will be the first to suffer. Oh it is
excellent To have a brute's strength; but it is
tyranny To use it like a beast.*

[Aside to ISABELLA] That was well said.

*Could great men throw thunderbolts
As the god Jove does, Jove would never be at
peace, For every little thing, a petty officer
Would use only this greatest weapon;
Nothing less! Merciful God,
You would rather with your lightning bolt
Split the unbreakable and hardned oak tree
Than the delicate myrtle tree: but man, a proud
man, Given a little bit of authority,
Absolutely unaware of what it is he's been
confident about, His unstable heart, like an
angry ape, Plays illusion tricks before high
heaven That make the angels weep; who if they
could laugh like humans
Would all laugh to death.*

LUCIO
[Aside to ISABELLA] O, to him, to him,
wench! He
will relent;
He's coming; I perceive 't.

[Aside to ISABELLA] Oh, go to him, go to him,
wench! He
will give in;
He's coming round; I can tell.

PROVOST
[Aside] Pray heaven she win him!

[Aside] Pray to God she wins him over!

ISABELLA
We cannot weigh our brother with ourself:
Great men may jest with saints; 'tis wit in them,
But in the less foul profanation.

We cannot judge others by the same standards
as ourselves; Great men may joke about saints;
it is witty from them, But in lesser men it is
blasphemy.

LUCIO
Thou'rt i' the right, girl; more o, that.

You are right about that, girl; more of that.

ISABELLA
That in the captain's but a choleric word,
Which in the soldier is flat blasphemy.

What from the captain is only an angry word,
From the soldier is downright profanity.

LUCIO
[Aside to ISABELLA] Art avised o' that? more
on 't.

[Aside to ISABELLA] Are you aware of this?
More about it.

ANGELO
Why do you put these sayings upon me?

Why do you make me listen to these sayings?

ISABELLA
Because authority, though it err like others,
Hath yet a kind of medicine in itself,
That skins the vice o' the top. Go to your bosom;
Knock there, and ask your heart what it doth
know
That's like my brother's fault: if it confess
A natural guiltiness such as is his,
Let it not sound a thought upon your tongue
Against my brother's life.

Because authority, thought it makes mistakes
like others, Still has a kind of healing power in
itself, That covers over wrong doings. Go to
you chest; Knock there, and ask you heart
whether it could think
Like my brother's did in his crime: if your heart
confesses A similar inherent tendency to that
guilt, Don't declare the words from your mouth
Against my brother's life.

ANGELO
[Aside] She speaks, and 'tis
Such sense, that my sense breeds with it. Fare
you well.

[Aside] She speaks, and it makes
So much sense, that I am aroused by it. Good
bye.

ISABELLA
Gentle my lord, turn back.

My gentle lord, change your mind.

ANGELO
I will bethink me: come again tomorrow.

I will think about it: come again tomorrow.

ISABELLA
Hark how I'll bribe you: good my lord, turn back.

Listen to how I will bribe you: my good lord, change your mind.

ANGELO
How! bribe me?

How! Bribe me?

ISABELLA
Ay, with such gifts that heaven shall share with you.

Yes, with the kind of gifts that heaven with share with you.

LUCIO
[Aside to ISABELLA] You had marr'd all else.

[Aside to ISABELLA] You would have made a mistake to offer anything else.

ISABELLA
Not with fond shekels of the tested gold,
Or stones whose rates are either rich or poor
As fancy values them; but with true prayers
That shall be up at heaven and enter there
Ere sun-rise, prayers from preserved souls,
From fasting maids whose minds are dedicate
To nothing temporal.

Not with foolish coins of tested gold, Or the jewels whose value are either rich or poor As they are valued on a whim; but with constant prayers That shall go to heaven and enter there Before the sunrise, prayers from the protected souls, From the nuns whose minds are dedicated To nothing world.

ANGELO
Well; come to me to-morrow.

Well; come to me tomorrow.

LUCIO
[Aside to ISABELLA] Go to; 'tis well; away!

[Aside to ISABELLA] Go on; all is well; go away!

ISABELLA
Heaven keep your honour safe!

Heaven keep your honor safe!

ANGELO
[Aside] Amen:
For I am that way going to temptation,
Where prayers cross.

[Aside] Amen: For I am going the way towards temptation, Where prayers conflict with one another.

ISABELLA
At what hour to-morrow
Shall I attend your lordship?

At what time tomorrow Should I visit your lordship?

ANGELO

At any time 'fore noon.

ISABELLA
'Save your honour!

ANGELO
From thee, even from thy virtue!
What's this, what's this? Is this her fault or
mine?
The tempter or the tempted, who sins most?
Ha!
Not she: nor doth she tempt: but it is I
That, lying by the violet in the sun,
Do as the carrion does, not as the flower,
Corrupt with virtuous season. Can it be
That modesty may more betray our sense
Than woman's lightness? Having waste ground
enough,
Shall we desire to raze the sanctuary
And pitch our evils there? O, fie, fie, fie!
What dost thou, or what art thou, Angelo?
Dost thou desire her foully for those things
That make her good? O, let her brother live!
Thieves for their robbery have authority
When judges steal themselves. What, do I love
her,
That I desire to hear her speak again,
And feast upon her eyes? What is't I dream on?
O cunning enemy, that, to catch a saint,
With saints dost bait thy hook! Most dangerous
Is that temptation that doth goad us on
To sin in loving virtue: never could the
strumpet,
With all her double vigour, art and nature,
Once stir my temper; but this virtuous maid
Subdues me quite. Even till now,
When men were fond, I smiled and wonder'd
how.

At any time before noon.

God save your honor!

Exeunt ISABELLA, LUCIO, and PROVOST

From you, even with your virtue!
Why, why? Is it her fault or mine?
The one who tempts, or the one who is tempted,
who sins most?
Ha!
It is not her: nor does she tempt: but it is I
Who, lying by the flower of chastity in the sun,
Do as the dead does, and not as the flower,
Corrupt by the wrong sun for virtue to flourish.
Can it be That chastity is more against our
nature Than a woman's promiscuity? Having
enough wasteland,
Do we want to burn down the holy place
And build up our evils there? Oh, for shame, for
shame for shame! What do you do, or what are
you, Angelo? Do you want her immorally for the
things That make her good? Oh, let her brother
live! Thieves have authority for their robbery
When judges also steal. Is it because I love her,
That I want to hear her speak again,
And look upon her eyes? What is it that I want?
Oh, cunning devil, who, in order to catch a
saint,
Baits the hook with a saint! Most dangerous
Is the temptation that makes us want
To sin because of loving virtue: never could a
woman,
With all her power doubled, with art and nature,
Once disturb my balanced temperament; but this
virtuous young lady Completely overpowers me.
Until now, When men were in love, I smiled and
wondered how.

Exit

SCENE III. A room in a prison.

Enter, severally, DUKE VINCENTIO disguised as a friar, and PROVOST

DUKE VINCENTIO
Hail to you, provost! so I think you are.

Hello, provost! As I think that's who you are.

PROVOST
I am the provost. What's your will, good friar?

I am the provost. What is it you want good friar?

DUKE VINCENTIO
Bound by my charity and my blest order,
I come to visit the afflicted spirits
Here in the prison. Do me the common right
To let me see them and to make me know
The nature of their crimes, that I may minister
To them accordingly.

Required by my good will and my religious order, I have come to visit those in distress Here in prison. Do me the right of a priestly visit And let me see them and let me know The kind of crimes they committed, that I may attend To them accordingly.

PROVOST
I would do more than that, if more were needful.

I would do more than just that, if more were necessary.

Enter JULIET

Look, here comes one: a gentlewoman of mine,
Who, falling in the flaws of her own youth,
Hath blister'd her report: she is with child;
And he that got it, sentenced; a young man
More fit to do another such offence
Than die for this.

Look, here comes one: a gentlewoman in my charge, Who, falling to the temptation of passion of her youth, Has ruined her reputation: she is pregnant; And he that got her pregnant, is sentenced; a young man, Who is more suitable to commit the offence again Than to die for it.

DUKE VINCENTIO
When must he die?

When will he die?

PROVOST
As I do think, to-morrow.
I have provided for you: stay awhile,

I think it is tomorrow, I have provided a space for you: stay here for a while.

To JULIET

And you shall be conducted.

And you shall be escorted.

DUKE VINCENTIO
Repent you, fair one, of the sin you carry?

Do you repent, young lady, for the sin you

JULIET
I do; and bear the shame most patiently.

DUKE VINCENTIO
I'll teach you how you shall arraign your conscience,
And try your penitence, if it be sound,
Or hollowly put on.
Or shown sincerely.

JULIET
I'll gladly learn.

DUKE VINCENTIO
Love you the man that wrong'd you?

JULIET
Yes, as I love the woman that wrong'd him.

DUKE VINCENTIO
So then it seems your most offenceful act
Was mutually committed?

JULIET
Mutually.

DUKE VINCENTIO
Then was your sin of heavier kind than his.

JULIET
I do confess it, and repent it, father.

DUKE VINCENTIO
'Tis meet so, daughter: but lest you do repent,
As that the sin hath brought you to this shame,
Which sorrow is always towards ourselves, not heaven,
Showing we would not spare heaven as we love it,
But as we stand in fear,--

JULIET
I do repent me, as it is an evil,
And take the shame with joy.

committed?

I do; and I endure the shame very patiently.

I'll teach you how you can question your conscience,
And test you atonement, to see if it is real,
_____
_____

I'll gladly learn.

Do you love the man that impregnated you?

Yes, as much as I love the woman that he impregnated, that is myself.

So then it seems your very offensive act
Was committed together by the two of you?

Together.

Then you sin was of a more severe kind than his.

I do confess it, and repent it, father.

It is proper that you do, daughter: but in case you do repent, Because the sin has brought you to this shame, In which the sorrow be feel is selfish, and not heavenly repentance,
Showing the we would not repent because we love God,
But because we fear him,--

I do repent my sin, as it is an evil,
And receive the shame from my actions with joy.

DUKE VINCENTIO
There rest.
Your partner, as I hear, must die to-morrow,
And I am going with instruction to him.
Grace go with you, Benedicite!

Maintain that attitude.
Your partner, I hear, is to die tomorrow,
And I am going to him with guidance.
Grace be with you, and bless you!

Exit

JULIET
Must die to-morrow! O injurious love,
That respites me a life, whose very comfort
Is still a dying horror!

He is to die tomorrow! Oh, hurtful love,
That give me life, whose very comfort
Is constantly a dying horror.

PROVOST
'Tis pity of him.

He is to be pitied.

Exeunt

SCENE IV. A room in ANGELO's house.

Enter ANGELO

ANGELO
When I would pray and think, I think and pray
To several subjects. Heaven hath my empty
words;
Whilst my invention, hearing not my tongue,
Anchors on Isabel: Heaven in my mouth,
As if I did but only chew his name;
And in my heart the strong and swelling evil
Of my conception. The state, whereon I studied
Is like a good thing, being often read,
Grown fear'd and tedious; yea, my gravity,
Wherein--let no man hear me--I take pride,
Could I with boot change for an idle plume,
Which the air beats for vain. O place, O form,
How often dost thou with thy case, thy habit,
Wrench awe from fools and tie the wiser souls
To thy false seeming! Blood, thou art blood:
Let's write good angel on the devil's horn:
'Tis not the devil's crest.

When I have time to pray and think, I think and pray About various subject. Heaven has my empty words; While my thoughts do not hear my words But fix solely on Isabel: God in my mouth, Like I am only chewing his name; And in my heart the strong and swelling evil Of my plan. The affairs of government, which I studied It like a good thing, it is often read, That has grown tired and tedious; yes, my authority, In which—I hope no one hears this—I take pride, If only I could, keeping my advantage, exchange it for a feathered hat, Which the air beats for no purpose. Oh social rank, oh ceremony, How often do you with your outward appearance, Inspire wonder from fools and blind even the wiser souls Into trusting your fake security! Desire, you are only desire: Even if we were to write the words 'good angel' on the devil's horn: It would not change the devil's nature.

Enter a SERVANT

How now! who's there?

What's going on! Who's there?

SERVANT
One Isabel, a sister, desires access to you.

Isabel, a nun, would like to speak to you.

ANGELO
Teach her the way.

Show her the way.

Exit SERVANT

O heavens!
Why does my blood thus muster to my heart,
Making both it unable for itself,
And dispossessing all my other parts
Of necessary fitness?
So play the foolish throngs with one that

Oh heavens! Why does my blood run to my heart, Making it both incapable itself, And depriving all my other parts Of the blood they need? Just as the foolish crowd do with one who

swoons;
Come all to help him, and so stop the air
By which he should revive: and even so
The general, subject to a well-wish'd king,
Quit their own part, and in obsequious fondness
Crowd to his presence, where their untaught love
Must needs appear offence.

How now, fair maid?

ISABELLA
I am come to know your pleasure.

ANGELO
That you might know it, would much better please me
Than to demand what 'tis. Your brother cannot live.

ISABELLA
Even so. Heaven keep your honour!

ANGELO
Yet may he live awhile; and, it may be,
As long as you or I
yet he must die.

ISABELLA
Under your sentence?

ANGELO
Yea.

ISABELLA
When, I beseech you? that in his reprieve,
Longer or shorter, he may be so fitted
That his soul sicken not.

ANGELO
Ha! fie, these filthy vices! It were as good
To pardon him that hath from nature stolen
A man already made, as to remit

---

faints;
Everyone comes to help him, and by doing so keep him from getting the air He needs to revive himself: and even so The people, subject to a well liked king, Stop doing their part, and with flattering affection Crowd around him, where their ignorant love
Seems to be an attack.

Enter ISABELLA

What is it, young lady?

I have come to know what you desire.

I would much rather that you would give me my desire,
Than asking what it is. Your brother cannot live.

So be it. Heaven keep you, your honor!

Still he could live a little while; and, it could be As long as you or I could live except he must die

Because you sentence him to death?

Yes.

When will it be, I ask you? So that in the time before his execution, Whether it be longer or shorter, he may be spiritually prepared So that his soul does not sicken at death.

Ha! For shame, these filthy sins! It was as good To pardon him who has murdered A man as to pardon The desirous pleasures of

Their saucy sweetness that do coin heaven's image
In stamps that are forbid: 'tis all as easy
Falsely to take away a life true made
As to put metal in restrained means
To make a false one.

forging a false coin With God's image: it is all as easy
To wrongly take away a life legitimately made
As to put metal in a counterfeit mold
To make a false coin.

ISABELLA
'Tis set down so in heaven, but not in earth.

Those crimes may be judged the same in heaven, but not in life.

ANGELO
Say you so? then I shall pose you quickly.
Which had you rather, that the most just law
Now took your brother's life; or, to redeem him,
Give up your body to such sweet uncleanness
As she that he hath stain'd?

Do you think so? Then I shall question you quickly. Which would you rather, that the very just law Took your brother's life now; or, to save him, You give up your body to the same pleasurable sin As the woman that your brother sullied.

ISABELLA
Sir, believe this,
I had rather give my body than my soul.

Sir, believe this,
I would rather give up my body than my soul.

ANGELO
I talk not of your soul: our compell'd sins
Stand more for number than for account.

I am not talking of your soul: our necessary sins Are there more to be counted than to be punished.

ISABELLA
How say you?

Where do you get that?

ANGELO
Nay, I'll not warrant that; for I can speak
Against the thing I say. Answer to this:
I, now the voice of the recorded law,
Pronounce a sentence on your brother's life:
Might there not be a charity in sin
To save this brother's life?

No, I won't stand up for that; for I can say something Contrary to what I said. Answer this: I, who am the voice of the law as it is written, Pronounce a sentence on your brother demanding his life for his crime: Couldn't there be a sin that could be committed To save your brother's life?

ISABELLA
Please you to do't,
I'll take it as a peril to my soul,
It is no sin at all, but charity.
It isn't a sin at all, but a kindness.

If you want to do it,
I'll risk the punishment of my soul.
_____
_____

ANGELO
Pleased you to do't at peril of your soul,
Were equal poise of sin and charity.

If you want to do it at the peril of your soul,
It about be a balance of sin and kindness.

ISABELLA

That I do beg his life, if it be sin,
Heaven let me bear it! you granting of my suit,
If that be sin, I'll make it my morn prayer
To have it added to the faults of mine,
And nothing of your answer.

*I am begging for his life, and if that is a sin
Heaven let me commit it! If you granting my
request Is a sin, I'll make it my morning prayer
That it be added to my sins,
And not be your responsibility.*

ANGELO

Nay, but hear me.
Your sense pursues not mine: either you are ignorant,
Or seem so craftily; and that's not good.

*No, but listen to me.
You are not understanding me: either you are
unaware what I am saying Or are cleverly
pretending to be so; and that's not good*

ISABELLA

Let me be ignorant, and in nothing good,
But graciously to know I am no better.

*Let me be unaware, and not good at all,
But with humility know I am no better.*

ANGELO

Thus wisdom wishes to appear most bright
When it doth tax itself; as these black masks
Proclaim an enshield beauty ten times louder
Than beauty could, display'd. But mark me;
To be received plain, I'll speak more gross:
Your brother is to die.

*That is how wisdom tries to seem very clever
When it admonishes itself; as when nuns
Proclaim a concealed beauty ten times greater
Than beauty could be displayed. But pay
attention; To be understood plainly, I'll speak
more bluntly: You brother is going to die.*

ISABELLA

So.

That is so.

ANGELO

And his offence is so, as it appears,
Accountant to the law upon that pain.

*And his offence is such that, as it appears,
It is accountable to the law with that penalty.*

ISABELLA

True.

True.

ANGELO

Admit no other way to save his life,--
As I subscribe not that, nor any other,
But in the loss of question,--that you, his sister,
Finding yourself desired of such a person,
Whose credit with the judge, or own great place,
Could fetch your brother from the manacles
Of the all-building law; and that there were
No earthly mean to save him, but that either
To this supposed, or else to let him suffer;

*Suppose there is no other way to save his life,--
As I agree to neither that, nor any other,
Except for the lack of better words,--that you,
his sister, Finding that you are desired by such a
person, Whose influence with the judge, or
whose own powerful position, Could free your
brother from the handcuffs Of the law on which
everything is founded; and that there were No
other way to save him, except either You must*

What would you do?

surrender your virginity To this hypothetical authority figure, or else your brother will suffer; What would you do?

ISABELLA
As much for my poor brother as myself:
That is, were I under the terms of death,
The impression of keen whips I'ld wear as rubies,
And strip myself to death, as to a bed
That longing have been sick for, ere I'ld yield
My body up to shame.

I would do the same for my poor brother as I would for myself: That is, if I were under the sentence of death, I would wear the marks of the biting whips as rubies, And bind myself to death, like I would to a bed That I have been longing, before I would yield My body up to shame.

ANGELO
Then must your brother die.

Then your brother must die.

ISABELLA
And 'twere the cheaper way:
Better it were a brother died at once,
Than that a sister, by redeeming him,
Should die for ever.

And it would be the less harmful way: It is better for a brother to die once, Than for a sister, by saving him, To suffer eternal damnation.

ANGELO
Were not you then as cruel as the sentence
That you have slander'd so?

Would that not make you as cruel as the sentence That you have spoken out against.

ISABELLA
Ignomy in ransom and free pardon
Are of two houses: lawful mercy
Is nothing kin to foul redemption.

Disgrace in buying freedom and freedom freely given Are two different things: legal mercy Is nothing like an evil exchange.

ANGELO
You seem'd of late to make the law a tyrant;
And rather proved the sliding of your brother
A merriment than a vice.

You just recently seemed to portray the law as a tyrant; And rather seemed to see the sinfulness of you brother As a light-hearted matter and as a crime.

ISABELLA
O, pardon me, my lord; it oft falls out,
To have what we would have, we speak not what we mean:
I something do excuse the thing I hate,
For his advantage that I dearly love.

Oh, forgive me, my lord: it often happens, In trying to get what we want, we don't say what we mean: I do somewhat make excuses for the thing I hate, For the advantage of the one whom I love dearly.

ANGELO
We are all frail.

We are all weak.

ISABELLA

Else let my brother die,
If not a feodary, but only he
Owe and succeed thy weakness.

ANGELO
Nay, women are frail too.

ISABELLA
Ay, as the glasses where they view themselves;
Which are as easy broke as they make forms.
Women! Help Heaven! men their creation mar
In profiting by them. Nay, call us ten times frail;
For we are soft as our complexions are,
And credulous to false prints.

ANGELO
I think it well:
And from this testimony of your own sex,--
Since I suppose we are made to be no stronger
Than faults may shake our frames,--let me be
bold;
I do arrest your words. Be that you are,
That is, a woman; if you be more, you're none;
If you be one, as you are well express'd
By all external warrants, show it now,
By putting on the destined livery.

ISABELLA
I have no tongue but one: gentle my lord,
Let me entreat you speak the former language.

ANGELO
Plainly conceive, I love you.

ISABELLA
My brother did love Juliet,
And you tell me that he shall die for it.

ANGELO
He shall not, Isabel, if you give me love.

ISABELLA
I know your virtue hath a licence in't,
Which seems a little fouler than it is,
To pluck on others.

Then let my brother die,
If he is not a servant to this weakness, and
instead it is he who solely Owns and inherits the
weakness that you speak of.

No, women are weak too.

Yes, as the mirrors where they view themselves;
Which are broken as easily as they reflect
images. Women! Heaven help them! Men ruin
their own power By abusing women. No, call us
ten times more week; For we are as soft as our
complexions, And believe in men's falsehoods.

I agree:
And this a statement speaking about your own
gender,-- Since I suggest we are made to be no
stronger Then the weaknesses we fall prey to,--
let me be blunt; I do take heed of your words.
Be what you are, That is, a woman; if you are
more than that, then you're not a woman;
If you are one, as you clearly seem to be
By your outward appearance, show it now,
By demonstrating women's weakness.

I do not tell lies: my gentle lord,
I ask you to speak plainly as you did before.

Plainly understand, I love you.

My brother did love Juliet,
And you tell me that he will die for it.

He will not, Isabel, if you give yourself over to
my love.

I know your goodness has an authority to it,
Which seems a little more horrible than it is,
In order to test others.

ANGELO

Believe me, on mine honour,
My words express my purpose.

ISABELLA

Ha! little honour to be much believed,
And most pernicious purpose! Seeming,
seeming!
I will proclaim thee, Angelo; look for't:
Sign me a present pardon for my brother,
Or with an outstretch'd throat I'll tell the world
aloud
What man thou art.

ANGELO

Who will believe thee, Isabel?
My unsoil'd name, the austereness of my life,
My vouch against you, and my place i' the state,
Will so your accusation overweigh,
That you shall stifle in your own report
And smell of calumny. I have begun,
And now I give my sensual race the rein:
Fit thy consent to my sharp appetite;
Lay by all nicety and prolixious blushes,
That banish what they sue for; redeem thy
brother
By yielding up thy body to my will;
Or else he must not only die the death,
But thy unkindness shall his death draw out
To lingering sufferance. Answer me to-morrow,
Or, by the affection that now guides me most,
I'll prove a tyrant to him. As for you,
Say what you can, my false o'erweighs your
true.

ISABELLA

To whom should I complain? Did I tell this,
Who would believe me? O perilous mouths,
That bear in them one and the self-same tongue,
Either of condemnation or approof;
Bidding the law make court'sy to their will:
Hooking both right and wrong to the appetite,
To follow as it draws! I'll to my brother:
Though he hath fallen by prompture of the
blood,
Yet hath he in him such a mind of honour.

Believe me, on my honor,
The words I say express what I want.

Ha! You have little honor to so believe,
And a terrible desire! Deception, deception!
I will accuse you, Angelo; look for it
Immediately sign me a pardon for my brother,
Or as loud as I can, I'll tell the whole world
What kind of man you are.

Who would believe you, Isabel?
My un-dirtied name, the strictness of my life,
My testimony against you, and my authority in
the governement, Will overpower your
accusations so much, That you will silence your
own story And seem like slander. I have begun,
And now I allow my desires to run freely:
Make your agreement fit my intense appetite:
Put aside all coyness and delaying blushes,
That send away what they ask for; save your
brother By giving up your body to my passion;
Or else me will not only die, But your refusal
will make his death so slow He lingers before
death and suffers. Answer me tomorrow Or, by
the desire that now guides me most, I will prove
myself a tyrant to him. As for you, Say what you
will, but my lies will overpower your truth.

Exit

Who could I tell this? If I told this to someone,
Who would believe me? Oh, terrible voices,
That can only tell truths,
Either of blame or approval;
Asking the law to go along with their desires:
Attaching both good and bad to the longing,
To follow along as it makes things up! I'll go to
my brother: Though he has fallen prey to the
urging of passion, Still he has in him an
honorable mind. I know, if he had twenty head

That, had he twenty heads to tender down
On twenty bloody blocks, he'ld yield them up,
Before his sister should her body stoop
To such abhorr'd pollution.
Then, Isabel, live chaste, and, brother, die:
More than our brother is our chastity.
I'll tell him yet of Angelo's request,
And fit his mind to death, for his soul's rest.

to lay down On twenty bloody blocks, he would give them up, Before his sister should give up her body To such terrible contamination. So, Isabel will live a virgin, and her brother will die: Our chastity is worth more than our brother. I'll tell him of Angelo's request, And prepare his mind for death, and his soul for heaven.

Exit

ACT III

SCENE I. A room in the prison.

Enter DUKE VINCENTIO disguised as before, CLAUDIO, and Provost

DUKE VINCENTIO
So then you hope of pardon from Lord
Angelo?

*So then you hope for a pardon from Lord
Angelo?*

CLAUDIO
The miserable have no other medicine
But only hope:
I've hope to live, and am prepared to die.

*Miserable people have no other medicine
Except hope:
I hope to live, but am prepared to die.*

DUKE VINCENTIO
Be absolute for death; either death or life
Shall thereby be the sweeter. Reason thus
with life:
If I do lose thee, I do lose a thing
That none but fools would keep: a breath
thou art,
Servile to all the skyey influences,
That dost this habitation, where thou keep'st,
Hourly afflict: merely, thou art death's fool;
For him thou labour'st by thy flight to shun
And yet runn'st toward him still. Thou art not
noble;
For all the accommodations that thou bear'st
Are nursed by baseness. Thou'rt by no means
valiant;
For thou dost fear the soft and tender fork
Of a poor worm. Thy best of rest is sleep,
And that thou oft provokest; yet grossly
fear'st
Thy death, which is no more. Thou art not
thyself;
For thou exist'st on many a thousand grains
That issue out of dust. Happy thou art not;
For what thou hast not, still thou strivest to
get,
And what thou hast, forget'st. Thou art not
certain;
For thy complexion shifts to strange effects,
After the moon. If thou art rich, thou'rt poor;
For, like an ass whose back with ingots bows,
Thou bear's thy heavy riches but a journey,

*Be set on for death; then either death or life
Will be sweeter. Reason with life like this:
If I lose you, I lose a thing
That no one but a fool wants to keep: you are
a breath
Servant to all the planetary influences
That this body where you are kept
Is troubled by hourly: you are entirely
death's fool;
You labor to try and run from him
And yet you still run towards him. You are
not noble;
Because all the comforts that you bring
Come from dishonorable beginnings. You are
by no means brave;
Because you fear the soft and tender forked
tongue Of a poor snake. Thy best way to rest
is sleep, And that you often produce; but
excessively fear
Your death, which is no more than sleep.
You are not yourself;
Because you exist in thousands of things
That grow from the earth. You are not
happy; Because what you don't have, you try
to get,
And what you have, you forget. You are not
consistant;
For your character changes in strange ways,
Taking after the moon. If you are rich, then
you are poor; Because, like a donkey whose
back is weighed down with gold bars You*

And death unloads thee. Friend hast thou none;
For thine own bowels, which do call thee sire,
The mere effusion of thy proper loins,
Do curse the gout, serpigo, and the rheum,
For ending thee no sooner. Thou hast nor youth nor age,
But, as it were, an after-dinner's sleep,
Dreaming on both; for all thy blessed youth
Becomes as aged, and doth beg the alms
Of palsied eld; and when thou art old and rich,
Thou hast neither heat, affection, limb, nor beauty,
To make thy riches pleasant. What's yet in this
That bears the name of life? Yet in this life
Lie hid moe thousand deaths: yet death we fear,
That makes these odds all even.

CLAUDIO
I humbly thank you.
To sue to live, I find I seek to die;
And, seeking death, find life: let it come on.

ISABELLA
[Within] What, ho! Peace here; grace and good company!

PROVOST
Who's there? come in: the wish deserves a welcome.

DUKE VINCENTIO
Dear sir, ere long I'll visit you again.

CLAUDIO
Most holy sir, I thank you.

ISABELLA
My business is a word or two with Claudio.

carry your heavy riches only on a journey, And death takes it away from you. You have no friends; Because your own children, who call you father,
The very product of your own lions,
Curse at sicknesses like gout, skin diseases and head colds For not ending you sooner.
You have neither youth nor age,
But instead an evening nap,
Dreaming of both; because all your blessed youth Becomes elderly, and begs for the riches Of old age; and when you are old and rich,
You have neither passion, nor love, nor an able body,
To make you riches pleasant. What's is still here
That is worth the name of life? Yet in this life More than a thousand deaths lie hidden: yet it is death that we fear,
That makes everything even.

I humbly thank you.
By begging to live, I find I seek to die;
And in seeking death I find life: let death come.

[Inside] Well, hello! I wish you peace, mercy and good company!

Who's there? Come in: the well-wishes deserve a welcome.

Dear sir, before long I'll visit you again.

Most holy sir, thank you.

Enter ISABELLA

I am here to have a word or two with Claudio.

PROVOST
And very welcome. Look, signior, here's
your sister.

DUKE VINCENTIO
Provost, a word with you.

PROVOST
As many as you please.

DUKE VINCENTIO
Bring me to hear them speak, where I may be
concealed.

CLAUDIO
Now, sister, what's the comfort?

ISABELLA
Why,
As all comforts are; most good, most good
indeed.
Lord Angelo, having affairs to heaven,
Intends you for his swift ambassador,
Where you shall be an everlasting leiger:
Therefore your best appointment make with
speed;
To-morrow you set on.

CLAUDIO
Is there no remedy?

ISABELLA
None, but such remedy as, to save a head,
To cleave a heart in twain.

CLAUDIO
But is there any?

ISABELLA
Yes, brother, you may live:
There is a devilish mercy in the judge,
If you'll implore it, that will free your life,
But fetter you till death.

CLAUDIO

And you're very welcome to do so. Look,
mister, here's your sister.

Provost, may I have a word with you?

You may have as many words as you please.

Bring me to where I may hear them speak but
not be seen.

Exeunt DUKE VINCENTIO and PROVOST

Now, sister, what's the consolation?

Why,
The same as all consolations are; very good,
very good indeed.
Lord Angelo has business with heaven,
And intends you to be his ambassador soon,
Where you will be an everlasting resident as
ambassador: Therefore you must make your
preparations quickly;
Tomorrow you leave for heaven.

Is there no solution?

None, but such a solution that would, in
order to save a head, Sever a heart in two.

But is there any?

Yes, brother, you may live:
The judge's mercy is evil,
If you'll take it, it will save your life,
But burden you till death.

Perpetual durance?

Life in prison?

ISABELLA

Ay, just; perpetual durance, a restraint,
Though all the world's vastidity you had,
To a determined scope.

Yes, exactly; live in prison, a restraint,
But with all the vastness of the world, you
will Be limited to a fixed reach.

CLAUDIO

But in what nature?

But what kind?

ISABELLA

In such a one as, you consenting to't,
Would bark your honour from that trunk you bear,
And leave you naked.

The kind that if you agreed to it,
Would strip your honor from your body,
And leave you naked.

CLAUDIO

Let me know the point.

Tell me what it is.

ISABELLA

O, I do fear thee, Claudio; and I quake,
Lest thou a feverous life shouldst entertain,
And six or seven winters more respect
Than a perpetual honour. Darest thou die?
The sense of death is most in apprehension;
And the poor beetle, that we tread upon,
In corporal sufferance finds a pang as great
As when a giant dies.

Oh, I am afraid of you, Claudio; and I shiver
with fright, That you might cherish your
feverish life, And might value six or seven
more year more Than you do continuous
honor. Do you fear death? The fearfulness of
death is mostly in anticipation; And the poor
bug that we step on, In bodily suffering
experiences a pain as great As when a giant
dies.

CLAUDIO

Why give you me this shame?
Think you I can a resolution fetch
From flowery tenderness? If I must die,
I will encounter darkness as a bride,
And hug it in mine arms.

Why do you shame me like this this?
Do you think I can find determination
In words of comfort? If I must die,
I will meet death's darkness as a bride,
And hug it in my arms.

ISABELLA

There spake my brother; there my father's grave
Did utter forth a voice. Yes, thou must die:
Thou art too noble to conserve a life
In base appliances. This outward-sainted deputy,
Whose settled visage and deliberate word
Nips youth i' the head and follies doth

My brother spoke; and my father's grave
Did utter a voice. Yes, you must die:
You are too noble to save a life
With a dishonorable solution. This
seemingly holy agent,
Whose unchanging appearance and carefully
calculated words
Grips youth by the head and with foolish acts

emmew
As falcon doth the fowl, is yet a devil
His filth within being cast, he would appear
A pond as deep as hell.

CLAUDIO
The prenzie Angelo!

ISABELLA
O, 'tis the cunning livery of hell,
The damned'st body to invest and cover
In prenzie guards! Dost thou think, Claudio?
If I would yield him my virginity,
Thou mightst be freed.

CLAUDIO
O heavens! it cannot be.

ISABELLA
Yes, he would give't thee, from this rank offence,
So to offend him still. This night's the time
That I should do what I abhor to name,
Or else thou diest to-morrow.

CLAUDIO
Thou shalt not do't.

ISABELLA
O, were it but my life,
I'ld throw it down for your deliverance
As frankly as a pin.

CLAUDIO
Thanks, dear Isabel.

ISABELLA
Be ready, Claudio, for your death tomorrow.

CLAUDIO
Yes. Has he affections in him,
That thus can make him bite the law by the nose,
When he would force it? Sure, it is no sin,
Or of the deadly seven, it is the least.

drives it into the water
As a falcon does with its prey, is still a devil;
If his filth were to be vomited up, he would
appear To be a pit as deep as hell.

The princely Angelo!

Oh, it's the cunning uniform of hell,
The most damned body to dress and cover
In princely embroidered clothes! Don't you
think so, Claudio? If I would give him my
virginity, You would be freed.

Oh heavens! It cannot be.

Yes, he would give it to you, with his own
terrible offence,
So you could continue to commit the crime.
This night is the time That I could do what I
detest to name, Or else you will die
tomorrow.

You will not do it.

Oh, If it was only my life,
I would throw it down for you freedom
As freely as a pin

Thanks dear Isabel.

Be ready, Claudio, for you death romorrow.

Yes, He does have lustful passions in him,
That force him to abuse the law,
When he is the one who enforeces it? Sure, it
is no sin,
Or at least out of the seven deadly sins, it is
the least.

ISABELLA
Which is the least?

Which is the least?

CLAUDIO
If it were damnable, he being so wise,
Why would he for the momentary trick
Be perdurably fined? O Isabel!

If it were so damnable, with him being so wise, Why would he, for just the momentary sexual tryst Be eternally punished? Oh, Isabel!

ISABELLA
What says my brother?

What are you saying, my brother?

CLAUDIO
Death is a fearful thing.

Death is a fearful thing.

ISABELLA
And shamed life a hateful.

And a shamed life is a hateful thing.

CLAUDIO
Ay, but to die, and go we know not where;
To lie in cold obstruction and to rot;
This sensible warm motion to become
A kneaded clod; and the delighted spirit
To bathe in fiery floods, or to reside
In thrilling region of thick-ribbed ice;
To be imprison'd in the viewless winds,
And blown with restless violence round about
The pendent world; or to be worse than worst
Of those that lawless and incertain thought
Imagine howling: 'tis too horrible!
The weariest and most loathed worldly life
That age, ache, penury and imprisonment
Can lay on nature is a paradise
To what we fear of death.

Yes, but to die and go somewhere we don't even know where it is; To lie in cold motionlessness and to rot; This feeling warm movement in life to become A lump of earth in death; and the spirit once capable of delight To bathe in fiery floods, or to reside In a extremely cold place of thick, ridged ice; To be imprisoned in the invisible winds, And be blown with restless violence around The world as it hangs; or to be worse than the worst Of those that terrible and uncertain thought Imagine howling: it's too horrible! The weariest and most hated life in this world The fact that age, pain, poverty and imprisonment Can be endured by human nature is a paradise In comparison to what we fear in death.

ISABELLA
Alas, alas!

Oh dear, oh dear!

CLAUDIO
Sweet sister, let me live:
What sin you do to save a brother's life,
Nature dispenses with the deed so far
That it becomes a virtue.

Sweet sister, let me live: What sin you commit in order to save your brother's life, Heavenly nature forgives the deed so much That it becomes a virtue.

ISABELLA

O you beast!
O faithless coward! O dishonest wretch!
Wilt thou be made a man out of my vice?
Is't not a kind of incest, to take life
From thine own sister's shame? What should
I think?
Heaven shield my mother play'd my father
fair!
For such a warped slip of wilderness
Ne'er issued from his blood. Take my
defiance!
Die, perish! Might but my bending down
Reprieve thee from thy fate, it should
proceed:
I'll pray a thousand prayers for thy death,
No word to save thee.

CLAUDIO
Nay, hear me, Isabel.

ISABELLA
O, fie, fie, fie!
Thy sin's not accidental, but a trade.
Mercy to thee would prove itself a bawd:
'Tis best thou diest quickly.

CLAUDIO
O hear me, Isabella!

DUKE VINCENTIO
Vouchsafe a word, young sister, but one
word.

ISABELLA
What is your will?

DUKE VINCENTIO
Might you dispense with your leisure, I
would by and
by have some speech with you: the
satisfaction I
would require is likewise your own benefit.

ISABELLA
I have no superfluous leisure; my stay must

Oh you beast!
You faithless coward! You dishonest wretch!
Will you be given life out of my sin?
Is that not a kind of incest, to take life
From your own sister's deflowering? What
should I think
Heaven forbid my mother was never
unfaithful to my father!
For such a wretched offspring
Never came from his blood. Take my
rejection!
Die, perish! If my payers might
Save you from your fate, you should still
suffer it.
I'll pray a thousand prayers for your death,
But not one for your life.

No, listen to me Isabel.

Oh shame on you! For shame!
Your sin is not an accident, but a habit.
Mercy given to you would turn into a whore:
It is best that you die quickly.

Oh listen to me, Isabella!

Re-enter DUKE VINCENTIO

Permit me to say a word, young sister, just
one word.

What is it?

Might you give me a moment of our time, I
would like to soon
Talk to you: what I am looking for
Is also to your benefit.

I have no extra time; my time must be

be
stolen out of other affairs; but I will attend you awhile.

DUKE VINCENTIO
Son, I have overheard what hath passed between you
and your sister. Angelo had never the purpose to
corrupt her; only he hath made an essay of her
virtue to practise his judgment with the disposition
of natures: she, having the truth of honour in her,
hath made him that gracious denial which he is most
glad to receive. I am confessor to Angelo, and I
know this to be true; therefore prepare yourself to
death: do not satisfy your resolution with hopes
that are fallible: tomorrow you must die; go to
your knees and make ready.

CLAUDIO
Let me ask my sister pardon. I am so out of love
with life that I will sue to be rid of it.

DUKE VINCENTIO
Hold you there: farewell.

Provost, a word with you!

PROVOST
What's your will, father

DUKE VINCENTIO
That now you are come, you will be gone.

Taken out of other business; but I will wait for you a while.

Walks apart

Son, I overheard what was said between you
And your sister. Angelo never had the intention to
Corrupt her; he only meant to make a test of her
Virtue to practice his judge of character:
She, having a truly honorable nature,
Gave him the virtuous denial which he was quite
Glad to receive. Angelo tells me his confessions, and I
Know this is true; so prepare yourself for
Death: do not preserve your determination with hopes
That are false: tomorrow you must die;
Kneel for prayer and make ready for death.

Let me as my sister's forgiveness. I am so tired
Of life that I will bed to be rid of it.

Keep that mindset: good bye.

Exit CLAUDIO

Provost, I would like a world with you!

Re-enter PROVOST

What is it, father?

Now that you are here, he should go away.

72

Leave me
awhile with the maid: my mind promises
with my
habit no loss shall touch her by my company.

PROVOST
In good time.

DUKE VINCENTIO
The hand that hath made you fair hath made
you good:
the goodness that is cheap in beauty makes
beauty
brief in goodness; but grace, being the soul of
your complexion, shall keep the body of it
ever
fair. The assault that Angelo hath made to
you,
fortune hath conveyed to my understanding;
and, but
that frailty hath examples for his falling, I
should
wonder at Angelo. How will you do to
content this
substitute, and to save your brother?

ISABELLA
I am now going to resolve him: I had rather
my
brother die by the law than my son should be
unlawfully born. But, O, how much is the
good duke
deceived in Angelo! If ever he return and I
can
speak to him, I will open my lips in vain, or
discover his government.

DUKE VINCENTIO
That shall not be much amiss: Yet, as the
matter
now stands, he will avoid your accusation; he
made
trial of you only. Therefore fasten your ear on
my
advisings: to the love I have in doing good a

Leave me
For a little while with the young lady: my
mind promises by my
Friar's habit that nothing shall harm her in
my company.

Very well.

Exit PROVOST. ISABELLA comes forward

The hand that created you beautiful also
created you virtuous:
Those who are beautiful but lacking in virtue
make their beauty
Short-lived; but divine virtue, being the
center of Your character, shall keep the rest
of it always
Beautiful. The proposition that Angelo made
to you
I have fortunately been made aware of; and,
except
That there are other examples of such bad
behavior, I would
Be astonished at Angelo. What will you do to
make Angelo happy,
And save your brother?

I am going to answer him: I would rather my
Brother die by the law than have my son be
Born out of marriage. But, oh, how much the
good duke
Has been deceived by Angelo! If he ever
returns and I can
Speak with him, I will tell him about it either
futilely or
expose his misconduct as governor.

That would not be wrong to do: yet, as the
matter
now stands, he will deny your accusation; he
made
The proposition only to you. So listen to my
Advice: from the joy I take in doing good, I
Thought of a solution. I am sure

remedy presents itself. I do make myself believe
that you may most uprighteously do a poor wronged
lady a merited benefit; redeem your brother from
the angry law; do no stain to your own gracious
person; and much please the absent duke, if
peradventure he shall ever return to have hearing of
this business.

That you can righteously do a poor, wronged
Lady a good favor; redeem your brother from
The angry law; commit no sin to dishonor your virutous
Character; and please the absent duke, if
Perhaps he should ever return to hear of
This business.

ISABELLA
Let me hear you speak farther. I have spirit to do
anything that appears not foul in the truth of my spirit.

Let me hear what you have to say. I have the courage to do
Anything that doesn't seem bad to my good nature.

DUKE VINCENTIO
Virtue is bold, and goodness never fearful. Have
you not heard speak of Mariana, the sister of
Frederick the great soldier who miscarried at sea?

Virtue is brave, and goodness is never fearful. Have
You not heard of Mariana, the sister of
Frederick the great soldier who had an accident at sea?

ISABELLA
I have heard of the lady, and good words went with her name.

I have hear of the lady, and good things were said about her.

DUKE VINCENTIO
She should this Angelo have married; was affianced
to her by oath, and the nuptial appointed: between
which time of the contract and limit of the solemnity, her brother Frederick was wrecked at sea,
having in that perished vessel the dowry of his
sister. But mark how heavily this befell to the
poor gentlewoman: there she lost a noble and
renowned brother, in his love toward her ever most
kind and natural; with him, the portion and

She was supposed to marry Angelo; they were betrothed
By oath, and the wedding arranged: between
The time of the engagement and the date
Of the ceremony, her brother Frederick was wrecked at sea,
And had in the sunken ship the dowry of his
Sister. But listen how gravely this affected the
Poor lady: she lost her noble and
Famous brother, who had always had love for her that was
Kind and brotherly; and with him the amount and basis

sinew of
her fortune, her marriage-dowry; with both, her
combinate husband, this well-seeming Angelo.

ISABELLA
Can this be so? did Angelo so leave her?

DUKE VINCENTIO
Left her in her tears, and dried not one of them
with his comfort; swallowed his vows whole,
pretending in her discoveries of dishonour: in few,
bestowed her on her own lamentation, which she yet
wears for his sake; and he, a marble to her tears,
is washed with them, but relents not.

ISABELLA
What a merit were it in death to take this poor maid
from the world! What corruption in this life, that
it will let this man live! But how out of this can she avail?

DUKE VINCENTIO
It is a rupture that you may easily heal: and the
cure of it not only saves your brother, but keeps
you from dishonour in doing it.

ISABELLA
Show me how, good father.

DUKE VINCENTIO
This forenamed maid hath yet in her the continuance
of her first affection: his unjust unkindness, that
in all reason should have quenched her love, hath,

Of her wealth, her marriage-dowry; with both gone, she also lost
Her fiancé, the seemingly good Angelo.

Did this really happen? Angelo left her?

Left her in her tears and didn't dry a single one
By comforting her; renounced all his vows,
And pretending he discovered that she was not sexually pure: in short,
He married her to her grief, which she still
Shows to him; and he, unmoved by her tears
Is washed in them, but never gives in.

What a good thing it would be for death to take this poor woman
From the world! What corruption there is in life, that
It allows this man to live! But how can she benefit out of our business?

It is a break up that you could easily heal: and the
Cure for it not only save your brother, but keeps
You from losing your virginity as well.

Show me how this is, good father.

The woman I mentioned continues to
Love Angelo: his unjust cruelty, that
Reasonably should have stopped her love, has instead
Like an obstacle in a stream, made it more
Forceful and uncontrollable. Go to Angelo;

like an impediment in the current, made it more
violent and unruly. Go you to Angelo;
answer his
requiring with a plausible obedience; agree with
his demands to the point; only refer yourself to
this advantage, first, that your stay with him may
not be long; that the time may have all shadow and
silence in it; and the place answer to convenience.
This being granted in course,--and now follows
all,--we shall advise this wronged maid to stead up
your appointment, go in your place; if the encounter
acknowledge itself hereafter, it may compel him to
her recompense: and here, by this, is your brother
saved, your honour untainted, the poor Mariana
advantaged, and the corrupt deputy scaled. The maid
will I frame and make fit for his attempt. If you
think well to carry this as you may, the doubleness
of the benefit defends the deceit from reproof.
What think you of it?

ISABELLA
The image of it gives me content already; and I
trust it will grow to a most prosperous perfection.

DUKE VINCENTIO
It lies much in your holding up. Haste you speedily

answer his
Request with a believable agreement; agree with
His demands exactly; only ask for conditions that are to your
Advantage, first, that your time with him will
Not be long; that it will be at a time that is dark and
Quiet; and that the place be convenient for you.
After this is granted,--and now this is how it works,--
We shall ask the woman who was wronged to carry out
You appointment, to go in your place; if the meeting
Is revealed afterwards, it would force him to
Set her situation to rights: and here, by this, is your brother
Saved, you honor untainted, the poor Mariana
Benefits, and the corrupt official judged. I will
Prepare the lady and ready her for his efforts. If you
Think you can manage this, the two-fold nature
Of the benefits defend the deception from blame.
What do you think of it?

The idea of it makes me happy already; and I
Trust that it will continue to a most successful completion.

It requires your ability to keep it up. Hurry now

to Angelo: if for this night he entreat you to his

bed, give him promise of satisfaction. I will presently to Saint Luke's: there, at the moated grange, resides this dejected Mariana. At that place call upon me; and dispatch with Angelo, that

it may be quickly.

ISABELLA
I thank you for this comfort. Fare you well, good father.

To Angelo: if he asks you to come tonight to his

Bed, promise him that you will. I will Now go to Saint Luke's: there, at the farmhouse with a moat, Is where the heartbroken Mariana lives. At that place you come meet with me; and make arrangements with Angelo, that It may be soon.

Thank you for this piece of mind. Good bye, good father.

Exeunt severally

SCENE II. The street before the prison.

Enter, on one side, DUKE VINCENTIO disguised as before; on the other, ELBOW, and Officers with POMPEY

ELBOW
Nay, if there be no remedy for it, but that you will
needs buy and sell men and women like beasts, we
shall have all the world drink brown and white bastard.

No, if there is no solution for it, except that you will
Need to buy and sell men and women like beasts, we
Will have everyone in the world drink Spanish wine.

DUKE VINCENTIO
O heavens! what stuff is here

Oh heavens! What nonsense is going on here?

POMPEY
'Twas never merry world since, of two usuries, the
merriest was put down, and the worser allowed by
order of law a furred gown to keep him warm; and
furred with fox and lamb-skins too, to signify, that
craft, being richer than innocency, stands for the facing.

It hasn't been a happy world since, out of two money schemes, the
The happier one was made illegal, and the worse one allowed by
The letter of the law a nice furred outfit to keep it warm; and
Furred with fox fur and lam-skin too, to show which
Scheme, being richer than innocence, shows off for the world.

ELBOW
Come your way, sir. 'Bless you, good father friar.

Come along, sir. Bless you, good father friar.

DUKE VINCENTIO
And you, good brother father. What offence hath
this man made you, sir?

And to you, good brother father. What offence has
This man committed, sir?

ELBOW
Marry, sir, he hath offended the law: and, sir, we
take him to be a thief too, sir; for we have found
upon him, sir, a strange picklock, which we have
sent to the deputy.

By the Virgin Mary, sir, he has committed crime: and, sir, we Believe him to be a thief as well, sir, for we found On his person, sir, a strange lock pick, which we have
Sent to the Governor.

DUKE VINCENTIO

Fie, sirrah! a bawd, a wicked bawd!
The evil that thou causest to be done,
That is thy means to live. Do thou but think
What 'tis to cram a maw or clothe a back
From such a filthy vice: say to thyself,
From their abominable and beastly touches
I drink, I eat, array myself, and live.
Canst thou believe thy living is a life,
So stinkingly depending? Go mend, go mend.

POMPEY
Indeed, it does stink in some sort, sir; but yet,
sir, I would prove—

DUKE VINCENTIO
Nay, if the devil have given thee proofs for sin,
Thou wilt prove his. Take him to prison, officer:
Correction and instruction must both work
Ere this rude beast will profit.

ELBOW
He must before the deputy, sir; he has given him
warning: the deputy cannot abide a
whoremaster: if
he be a whoremonger, and comes before him, he
were
as good go a mile on his errand.

DUKE VINCENTIO
That we were all, as some would seem to be,
From our faults, as faults from seeming, free!

ELBOW
His neck will come to your waist,--a cord, sir.

POMPEY
I spy comfort; I cry bail. Here's a gentleman and
a
friend of mine.

LUCIO
How now, noble Pompey! What, at the wheels
of
Caesar? art thou led in triumph? What, is there
none of Pygmalion's images, newly made

Shame on you, man! A procurer, a wicker
procurer of whores! The evil that you make
happen Is you means of making a living. Do
you think about What it means to feed a belly
and cloth a back From such a filthy sin: say to
yourself, From the whore's horrible and beastly
touches I drink, I eat, I dress myself, and I live.
Can you believe your living is a life,
Supported so hideously? Go make amends, go
make amends.

Indeed, it is somewhat hideous, sir; but still,
Sir, I would prove--

No, if the devil has given you evidence for sin,
You will prove his sin. Take him to prison,
officer: Punishment and instruction most both
work on him Berfore this lowly man will benefit
from it.

He must go before the Governor, sir; he has
given him A warning: the deputy cannot tolerate
a whoremaster: if
There is a man who searches out whores, who
goes before him, he would
Rather be doing anything else than that.

If only we were all, as some would seem to be
Free from our faults, and faults from seeming
otherwise!

His neck will have a rope around it life your
belt, sir.

I see a good thing; I call out for bail money.
Here's a gentleman and a
Friend of mine.

Enter LUCIO

What's this, noble Pompey! You following
An officer like disgraced prisoners paraded
behind Caesar? Are there
No ideal women, young women, to be

woman, to be
had now, for putting the hand in the pocket and extracting it clutch'd? What reply, ha? What sayest thou to this tune, matter and method? Is't not drowned i' the last rain, ha? What sayest thou, Trot? Is the world as it was, man? Which is
the way? Is it sad, and few words? or how? The trick of it?

Had now, to put enough money in your pocket To grab a fistful? What's your answer, huh? What Do you say to these words, their meaning and reasoning? Is it All gone, huh? What do you say, Old boy? Is everything as it used to be, man? What is It now? Is it miserable? Or what? How Is it?

DUKE VINCENTIO
Still thus, and thus; still worse!

It's all the same; and worse!

LUCIO
How doth my dear morsel, thy mistress? Procures she
still, ha?

How is my little thing, your lady? Does she still find Whores, huh?

POMPEY
Troth, sir, she hath eaten up all her beef, and she is herself in the tub.

To be honest, sir, she has worn out all her whores, and she Is also suffering from venereal disease.

LUCIO
Why, 'tis good; it is the right of it; it must be so: ever your fresh whore and your powdered bawd:
an unshunned consequence; it must be so. Art going
to prison, Pompey?

Well, that's okay; it's the right thing to do; to must That way: always a fresh whore and a heavily made-up matron. An unavoidable result; it always happens that way. Are you going To prison, Pompey?

POMPEY
Yes, faith, sir.

Yes, it's true, sir.

LUCIO
Why, 'tis not amiss, Pompey. Farewell: go, say I sent thee thither. For debt, Pompey? or how?

Well, that's not wrong, Pompey. Good bye: go, say I Sent you there. For not paying your debts, Pompey? Or something?

ELBOW
For being a bawd, for being a bawd.

For being a procurer, a procurer of whores.

LUCIO
Well, then, imprison him: if imprisonment be the
due of a bawd, why, 'tis his right: bawd is he doubtless, and of antiquity too; bawd-born.

Well, then, take him to jail: if prison is the Punishment for a procurer, well then, that's what he gets: he is definitely A whore procurer, and has been for a long time;

Farewell, good Pompey. Commend me to the prison,
Pompey: you will turn good husband now, Pompey; you
will keep the house.

POMPEY
I hope, sir, your good worship will be my bail.

LUCIO
No, indeed, will I not, Pompey; it is not the wear.
I will pray, Pompey, to increase your bondage: If
you take it not patiently, why, your mettle is the more. Adieu, trusty Pompey. 'Bless you, friar.

DUKE VINCENTIO
And you.

LUCIO
Does Bridget paint still, Pompey, ha?

ELBOW
Come your ways, sir; come.

POMPEY
You will not bail me, then, sir?

LUCIO
Then, Pompey, nor now. What news abroad, friar?
what news?

ELBOW
Come your ways, sir; come.

LUCIO
Go to kennel, Pompey; go.

What news, friar, of the duke?

DUKE VINCENTIO
I know none. Can you tell me of any?

born to be on. Good bye, good Pompey. Speak well of me in prison,
Pompey: you will become a good housekeeper now, Pompey; you
Will clean the house.

I was hoping good honorable sir, that you would bail be out.

No, indeed, I will not, Pompey; that's is not the way of things.
I will pray, Pompey, to lengthen your time in prison: if
You do not take it patiently, well then, your spirit Is strong. Farewell, loyal Pompey. Bless you, friar.

And you.

Does Bridget still wear a whore's makeup, Pompey, huh?

Come this way, sir; come on.

You won't bail me out, then, sir?

I said I wouldn't, Pompey, and I still won't. What's the news from elsewhere, friar? What's the news?

Come this way, sir; come on.

Go to prison, Pompey; go on.

Exeunt ELBOW, POMPEY and Officers

Is there any news, friar, of the duke?

I don't know any. Do you?

LUCIO
Some say he is with the Emperor of Russia; other
some, he is in Rome: but where is he, think you?

Some say he is with the Emperor of Russia; others
Say he is in Rome; but where do you think he is?

DUKE VINCENTIO
I know not where; but wheresoever, I wish him well.

I don't know where he is; but where ever it is, I wish him well.

LUCIO
It was a mad fantastical trick of him to steal from
the state, and usurp the beggary he was never born
to. Lord Angelo dukes it well in his absence; he puts transgression to 't.

It was a crazy bizarre idea of his to leave
The state, and take on a normal life that he was never born
Into. Lord Angelo governs well in his absence; he
Punishes people for their crimes.

DUKE VINCENTIO
He does well in 't.

He is good at it.

LUCIO
A little more lenity to lechery would do no harm in
him: something too crabbed that way, friar.

A little easygoingness towards sexual crimes wouldn't be a
Bad thing: he's a little too harsh with that, friar.

DUKE VINCENTIO
It is too general a vice, and severity must cure it.

That sin is too widespread, and harshness will fix that.

LUCIO
Yes, in good sooth, the vice is of a great kindred;
it is well allied: but it is impossible to extirp
it quite, friar, till eating and drinking be put
down. They say this Angelo was not made by man and
woman after this downright way of creation: is it true, think you?

Yes, in all honestly, that sin is committed by many people;
It has many followers: but it is impossible to get rid of It completely, friar, until eating and drinking are stopped as well. They say this Angelo was not created from a father and mother the way most babies are made: is that True, do you think?

DUKE VINCENTIO
How should he be made, then?

How else should he have been made, then?

LUCIO
Some report a sea-maid spawned him; some, that he
was begot between two stock-fishes. But it is

Some say he was born from a mermaid; some, that he
Was conceived from two common fish. But it is

certain that when he makes water his urine is
congealed ice; that I know to be true: and he is a
motion generative; that's infallible.

*Certain that when he urinates his pee is
Solid ice; that I know is true: and he is just a
A male puppet; that's the truth.*

DUKE VINCENTIO
You are pleasant, sir, and speak apace.

You are funny, sir, and speak quickly.

LUCIO
Why, what a ruthless thing is this in him, for the
rebellion of a codpiece to take away the life of a
man! Would the duke that is absent have done
this?
Ere he would have hanged a man for the getting
a
hundred bastards, he would have paid for the
nursing
a thousand: he had some feeling of the sport: he
knew the service, and that instructed him to
mercy.

*This is such a cruel thing that he's doing,
Taking a man's life for his penis acting out!
Would the absent duke have done this?
Before he would hand a man for having
A hundred children out of wedlock, he would
first have paid for the nurses
For a thousand: he had some understanding of
sexual passions: he
He knew the business of it, and that made him
merciful.*

DUKE VINCENTIO
I never heard the absent duke much detected for
women; he was not inclined that way.

*I never heard the absent duke accused of having
sex With women; he was not like that.*

LUCIO
O, sir, you are deceived.

Oh, sir, you are mistaken

DUKE VINCENTIO
'Tis not possible.

That's not possible

LUCIO
Who, not the duke? yes, your beggar of fifty;
and
his use was to put a ducat in her clack-dish: the
duke had crotchets in him. He would be drunk
too;
that let me inform you.

*What, the duke wasn't like that? Yes, a fifty-year
old beggar woman; and
he used to often put his gold-coin in her beggar
dish, if you know what I mean: the duke had
some strange ideas. He would drink too;
I'll tell you that*

DUKE VINCENTIO
You do him wrong, surely.

You have him all wrong, surely.

LUCIO
Sir, I was an inward of his. A shy fellow was the
duke: and I believe I know the cause of his
withdrawing.

*Sir, I was a close friend of his. He's a shy man,
The duke: and I believe I know the reason
He left.*

DUKE VINCENTIO
What, I prithee, might be the cause?

And what, I ask you, might be the cause?

LUCIO
No, pardon; 'tis a secret must be locked within the
teeth and the lips: but this I can let you
understand, the greater file of the subject held the
duke to be wise.

No I'm sorry; it's a secret that must be kept inside.
But I can tell you this,
Most of his subject believed the
Duke to be wise.

DUKE VINCENTIO
Wise! why, no question but he was.

Wise! Well, there's no question that he was.

LUCIO
A very superficial, ignorant, unweighing fellow.

That he was a very superficial, ignorant,
sexually loose man.

DUKE VINCENTIO
Either this is the envy in you, folly, or
mistaking:
the very stream of his life and the business he hath
helmed must upon a warranted need give him a better
proclamation. Let him be but testimonied in his own
bringings-forth, and he shall appear to the
envious a scholar, a statesman and a soldier.
Therefore you speak unskilfully: or if your
knowledge be more it is much darkened in your
malice.

Either you are mean-spirited, foolish, or
mistaken:
The very nature of his life and the business he
Lead must give him a better reputation if you
need proof
Let him be evaluated in his own
Achievements, and to the jealous scholar he will
Seem to be a statesman and a soldier
Therefore you speak without knowing the truth;
of if you
Know better it doesn't show through your
spitefulness.

LUCIO
Sir, I know him, and I love him.

Sir, I know him, and I love him.

DUKE VINCENTIO
Love talks with better knowledge, and
knowledge with
dearer love.

If you loved him you would know him better, and
if you had that knowledge
You would speak better about him.

LUCIO
Come, sir, I know what I know.

Come on, sir, I know what I know.

DUKE VINCENTIO
I can hardly believe that, since you know not

I can hardly believe that, since you don't know

what
you speak. But, if ever the duke return, as our
prayers are he may, let me desire you to make your
answer before him. If it be honest you have spoke,
you have courage to maintain it: I am bound to call
upon you; and, I pray you, your name?

LUCIO
Sir, my name is Lucio; well known to the duke.

DUKE VINCENTIO
He shall know you better, sir, if I may live to
report you.

LUCIO
I fear you not.

DUKE VINCENTIO
O, you hope the duke will return no more; or you
imagine me too unhurtful an opposite. But indeed I
can do you little harm; you'll forswear this again.

LUCIO
I'll be hanged first: thou art deceived in me,
friar. But no more of this. Canst thou tell if
Claudio die to-morrow or no?

DUKE VINCENTIO
Why should he die, sir?

LUCIO
Why? For filling a bottle with a tundish. I would
the duke we talk of were returned again: the
ungenitured agent will unpeople the province with
continency; sparrows must not build in his
house-eaves, because they are lecherous. The duke
yet would have dark deeds darkly answered; he would

what
You're talking about. But, if the duke ever
returns, as we Pray that we will, I want you to
put forth your
Comments in front of him. If what you have said
is true,
You will be brave enough to justify it: I am
going to ask
For you; and please tell me, what is your name?

Sir, my name is Luscio; the duke knows my
name well.

He will know you better than that, sir, if I live to
Tell him of you.

I'm not afraid of you.

Oh, you hope the duke won't return; or you
Think I am too weak an enemy. But truly I can't
Do you much harm; you'll deny this another
time.

I'll be hanged first: you have me mistaken,
Friar. But let's end this talk. Can you tell me if
Claudio is supposed to die tomorrow?

Why would he die, sir?

Why you ask? For filling a bottle with his long
rod, if you know what I mean, I wish the duke
we were talking about would come back: the
Sexless governor, Angelo, will lower the
population of the province with Abstinence;
Sparrows are forbidden to build their nests
under The edge of his roof, because they are
sexual, being Venus's sacred birds. The duke
Would have private sexual deeds privately dealt

never bring them to light: would he were
returned!
Marry, this Claudio is condemned for
untrussing.
Farewell, good friar: I prithee, pray for me. The
duke, I say to thee again, would eat mutton on
Fridays. He's not past it yet, and I say to thee,
he would mouth with a beggar, though she smelt
brown
bread and garlic: say that I said so. Farewell.

with; he would Never bring them out in the open
in: I wish he would come back!
By the Virgin Mary, Claudio is condmned for
undressing.
Good bye, good friar: I ask you to pray for me.
The Duke, I will say again, would eat lamb on
Friday against the law. He's not better than
that, and I tell you He would kiss a beggar, even
if she smelled of brown
Bread and garlic: tell him I said so. Good bye

Exit

DUKE VINCENTIO
No might nor greatness in mortality
Can censure 'scape; back-wounding calumny
The whitest virtue strikes. What king so strong
Can tie the gall up in the slanderous tongue?
But who comes here?

No mighty or highly moral person
Can escape criticism; painful slander
Strikes the purest virtue. What king is strong
enough To force people to no speak mean
words? But who is that?

Enter ESCALUS, PROVOST, and Officers with
MISTRESS OVERDONE

ESCALUS
Go; away with her to prison!

Go; take her away to prison!

MISTRESS OVERDONE
Good my lord, be good to me; your honour is
accounted
a merciful man; good my lord.

My good lord, be nice to me; you are considered
A merciful man; my good lord.

ESCALUS
Double and treble admonition, and still forfeit in
the same kind! This would make mercy swear
and play
the tyrant.

Two and three warnings, and you still commit
The same crime! This would make even mercy
itself fed up
And become ruthless.

PROVOST
A bawd of eleven years' continuance, may it
please
your honour.

A brothel matron of a whole eleven years time, if
you would like to know
Your honor.

MISTRESS OVERDONE
My lord, this is one Lucio's information against
me.
Mistress Kate Keepdown was with child by him
in the

My lord, Lucio spoke out against me.
Mistress Kate Keepdown was impregnated by
him when the
Duke was ruling; he promised her marriage: but

duke's time; he promised her marriage: his child
is a year and a quarter old, come Philip and
Jacob:
I have kept it myself; and see how he goes about
to abuse me!

ESCALUS
That fellow is a fellow of much licence: let him
be
called before us. Away with her to prison! Go
to;
no more words.

Provost, my brother Angelo will not be altered;
Claudio must die to-morrow: let him be
furnished
with divines, and have all charitable preparation.
if my brother wrought by my pity, it should not
be
so with him.

PROVOST
So please you, this friar hath been with him, and
advised him for the entertainment of death.

ESCALUS
Good even, good father.

DUKE VINCENTIO
Bliss and goodness on you!

ESCALUS
Of whence are you?

DUKE VINCENTIO
Not of this country, though my chance is now
To use it for my time: I am a brother
Of gracious order, late come from the See
In special business from his holiness.

ESCALUS
What news abroad i' the world?

DUKE VINCENTIO
None, but that there is so great a fever on

his child
Is a year and a quarter old, come May 1ˢᵗ:
I have raised it myself; and now he goes about
saying bad things about me!

That man is a very immoral man: we will
Call him to answer to us. Take her away to
prison! Go on;
Don't speak.

Exeunt Officers with MISTRESS OVERDONE

Provost, my colleague Angelo will not change
his mind; Claudio will die tomorrow: let him be
provided
With clergymen, and have his last rites.
If my colleague acted with my same pity, it
would not be
This way for him.

If it makes you happy, the friar has been with
him, and Prepared him for the acceptance of
death.

Well good then, good father.

Happiness and health for you!

Where are you from?

Not from this country, though I am living here
no for the time being: I am a brother
of a holy order, just recently come from the Holy
See in Rome On special business from his
holiness.

What's the news from the rest of the world?

None, except that righteousness has suck a

goodness, that the dissolution of it must cure it:
novelty is only in request; and it is as dangerous
to be aged in any kind of course, as it is virtuous
to be constant in any undertaking. There is
scarce
truth enough alive to make societies secure; but
security enough to make fellowships accurst:
much
upon this riddle runs the wisdom of the world.
This
news is old enough, yet it is every day's news. I
pray you, sir, of what disposition was the duke?

ESCALUS
One that, above all other strifes, contended
especially to know himself.

DUKE VINCENTIO
What pleasure was he given to?

ESCALUS
Rather rejoicing to see another merry, than
merry at
any thing which professed to make him rejoice:
a
gentleman of all temperance. But leave we him
to
his events, with a prayer they may prove
prosperous;
and let me desire to know how you find Claudio
prepared. I am made to understand that you have
lent him visitation.

DUKE VINCENTIO
He professes to have received no sinister
measure
from his judge, but most willingly humbles
himself
to the determination of justice: yet had he
framed
to himself, by the instruction of his frailty, many
deceiving promises of life; which I by my good
leisure have discredited to him, and now is he
resolved to die.

sickness That only death will cure it:
New fashions only come when in demand; and it
is dangerous To be behind the times in any
situation, as it is honorable To be steady in any
task. There is hardly
Enough truth left to make societies safe; but
Overconfidence enough to make trade
partnerships doomed to fail: much
Thinking is done by the wise of the world on
how to solve this problem. This
Is old news, but it is the same every day. I
Ask you sir, how is the duke's character?

Above all other activities, he attempts
Especially to know himself well.

What does he do to enjoy himself?

He'd be happier seeing another joyful, rather
than joyful at
Any thing that he said have him happiness: he's
a
Gentleman of great self-control. But let us leave
him to
His doings, with a prayer that they may turn out
well;
And I wish to know how well you think Claudio
Is prepared. I am told that you have
Visited him.

He claims to have received no unfair treatment
From his judge, but quite willingly cooperative
To the sentence of his punishment: but he had
come
Up with, due to the encouragement of his human
weakness, many
False promises of life; which in time
Showed him to be untrue, and now he is
Ready to die.

ESCALUS

You have paid the heavens your function, and the
prisoner the very debt of your calling. I have
laboured for the poor gentleman to the extremest
shore of my modesty: but my brother justice have I
found so severe, that he hath forced me to tell him
he is indeed Justice.

*You have done your heavenly duty, and the
Prisoner is the one you did it for. I have
worked for the poor gentleman to the limits
of my abilities: but I have found my colleagues
judgment
to be so hard, that he forced me to tell him
That he is Justice itself.*

DUKE VINCENTIO

If his own life answer the straitness of his
proceeding, it shall become him well; wherein if he
chance to fail, he hath sentenced himself.

*If he leads his own life with the strictness of his
Judgments, it will do him well; but if he
Happens to fail, he has already sentenced
himself.*

ESCALUS

I am going to visit the prisoner. Fare you well.

I am going to visit the prisoner. Good bye.

DUKE VINCENTIO

Peace be with you!

Peace be with you!

Exeunt ESCALUS and PROVOST

He who the sword of heaven will bear
Should be as holy as severe;
Pattern in himself to know,
Grace to stand, and virtue go;
More nor less to others paying
Than by self-offences weighing.
Shame to him whose cruel striking
Kills for faults of his own liking!
Twice treble shame on Angelo,
To weed my vice and let his grow!
O, what may man within him hide,
Though angel on the outward side!
How may likeness made in crimes,
Making practise on the times,
To draw with idle spiders' strings
Most ponderous and substantial things!
Craft against vice I must apply:
With Angelo to-night shall lie
His old betrothed but despised;
So disguise shall, by the disguised,
Pay with falsehood false exacting,

*He who bears the legal authoerity
Should be not only harsh but virtuous as well;
Setting the model himself,
Maintain himself honorably, and behave
righteously Passing no harder judgments on
others That he would on himself.
Shame on him, whose cruel blow
Kills a man for something he too is guilty of!
Twice and three times shame on Angelo,
To get rid of this sin and let another take it's
place! Oh, what a man may hide within himself,
Though outwardly he appears to be an angel!
Look how such seeming virtuousness is based in
crimes, Deceiving those around him,
To catch with mere delicate strings
Great and weighty seeming crimes!
I must use great skill against such wickedness:
Tonight Angelo shall sleep with
His scorned ex-fiance;
So trickery by the woman who is disguised,
Will repay his unfair demands with a scam,*

And perform an old contracting.   *And bind their marriage contract.*

Exit

ACT IV

SCENE I. The moated grange at ST. LUKE's.

Enter MARIANA and a Boy

Take, O, take those lips away,
That so sweetly were forsworn;
And those eyes, the break of day,
Lights that do mislead the morn:
But my kisses bring again, bring again;
Seals of love, but sealed in vain, sealed in vain.

MARIANA
Break off thy song, and haste thee quick away:
Here comes a man of comfort, whose advice
Hath often still'd my brawling discontent.

I cry you mercy, sir; and well could wish
You had not found me here so musical:
Let me excuse me, and believe me so,
My mirth it much displeased, but pleased my
woe.

DUKE VINCENTIO
'Tis good; though music oft hath such a charm
To make bad good, and good provoke to harm.
I pray, you, tell me, hath any body inquired
for me here to-day? much upon this time have
I promised here to meet.

MARIANA
You have not been inquired after:
I have sat here all day.

DUKE VINCENTIO
I do constantly believe you. The time is come
even
now. I shall crave your forbearance a little: may
be I will call upon you anon, for some advantage
to yourself.

Boy sings
Oh, take those lips away,
That were so sweetly withdrawn;
And those eyes, the break of day,
Lights that mislead the morning:
But my kisses bring again, bring again;
Promises of love, but promised in vain,
promised in vain.

Quite singing, and hurry away:
Here comes a man of guidance, whose adivce
Has often helped with my hostile unhappiness.

Exit Boy

Enter DUKE VINCENTIO disguised as before

I beg your pardon, sir; and wish
That you had not found me here singing:
Let me excuse myself, and believe me,
It did not humor me, but instead made me
regretful.

It is good; though music often has such a charm
To turn bad into good, and to make good cause
harm. Would you tell me, has anyone asked
For me here today? Around this time,
I promised to meet someone here.

You have not been asked for:
I have sat here all day.

Enter ISABELLA

I always believe you. The time has come
Now. I shall ask you to have a little patience:
maybe
I will ask for you later, about something that
will be to your advantage.

MARIANA
I am always bound to you.

I am always in your debt.

Exit

DUKE VINCENTIO
Very well met, and well come.
What is the news from this good deputy?

Well, hello and welcome
What do you have to tell me?

ISABELLA
He hath a garden circummured with brick,
Whose western side is with a vineyard back'd;
And to that vineyard is a planched gate,
That makes his opening with this bigger key:
This other doth command a little door
Which from the vineyard to the garden leads;
There have I made my promise
Upon the heavy middle of the night
To call upon him.

He was a garden walled around with brick,
Whose western side is backed with a vineyard;
With a planked gate leading into the vineyard,
That he can open with this bigger key:
And this other key opens a little door
Which leads from the vineyard to the garden;
I have promised
In the middle of the night
To meet him there.

DUKE VINCENTIO
But shall you on your knowledge find this way?

But will you be able to find your way?

ISABELLA
I have ta'en a due and wary note upon't:
With whispering and most guilty diligence,
In action all of precept, he did show me
The way twice o'er.

I have taken care and made note of the way:
In whispers and with guilty thoroughness,
With gestures, he did show me
The way twice.

DUKE VINCENTIO
Are there no other tokens
Between you 'greed concerning her observance?

And there are no other signs
That you agreed on, about what she must do?

ISABELLA
No, none, but only a repair i' the dark;
And that I have possess'd him my most stay
Can be but brief; for I have made him know
I have a servant comes with me along,
That stays upon me, whose persuasion is
I come about my brother.

No, none, but only to go into the dark;
And I have told him that I can only stay
For a little while; for I have told him
That I have a servant who will come with me,
And will wait for me, who believes that
I come about my brother.

DUKE VINCENTIO
'Tis well borne up.
I have not yet made known to Mariana
A word of this. What, ho! within! come forth!

It is a well made plan.
I have not yet told Mariana
A word of this. Hello! Come in here!

Re-enter MARIANA

I pray you, be acquainted with this maid;
She comes to do you good.

I would like you to meet this young lady;
She comes to help you.

ISABELLA
I do desire the like.

I do wish to do that.

DUKE VINCENTIO
Do you persuade yourself that I respect you?

Do you believe that I respect you?

MARIANA
Good friar, I know you do, and have found it.

Good friar, I know you do, and have seen it.

DUKE VINCENTIO
Take, then, this your companion by the hand,
Who hath a story ready for your ear.
I shall attend your leisure: but make haste;
The vaporous night approaches.

Then, take this woman by the hand,
Who has a story to tell you.
I will wait here for you to return: but hurry;
The misty night approaches.

MARIANA
Will't please you walk aside?

Would you like to walk aside?

Exeunt MARIANA and ISABELLA

DUKE VINCENTIO
O place and greatness! millions of false eyes
Are stuck upon thee: volumes of report
Run with these false and most contrarious quests
Upon thy doings: thousand escapes of wit
Make thee the father of their idle dreams
And rack thee in their fancies.

Oh, social rank and power! Millions of
treacherous eyes Stare at you: volumes of
statements Are full of these fake and
contradictory accounts About what you do: a
thousand witty comments Seek you in their idle
dreams And pester you in their fantasies.

Re-enter MARIANA and ISABELLA

Welcome, how agreed?

Welcome, did you come to an agreement?

ISABELLA
She'll take the enterprise upon her, father,
If you advise it.

She'll do it, father,
If you recommend it.

DUKE VINCENTIO
It is not my consent,
But my entreaty too.

I not only agree,
But ask for it aswell.

ISABELLA
Little have you to say

You don't have much to say, but

When you depart from him, but, soft and low,
'Remember now my brother.'

MARIANA
Fear me not.

DUKE VINCENTIO
Nor, gentle daughter, fear you not at all.
He is your husband on a pre-contract:
To bring you thus together, 'tis no sin,
Sith that the justice of your title to him
Doth flourish the deceit. Come, let us go:
Our corn's to reap, for yet our tithe's to sow.

When you leave him, soft and low, say
"Now, remember my brother."

Don't worry about me.

Nor should you, gentle daughter, worry at all.
He is you husband by your betrothal agreement:
To bring you together in this way, is not a sin,
Since the truthfulness of your relationship to
him Enhances the trickery. Come, let us go:
We will reap the reward, after we put in the
work.

Exeunt

SCENE II. A room in the prison.

Enter PROVOST and POMPEY

PROVOST
Come hither, sirrah. Can you cut off a man's head?

Come here, man. Can you cut of a man's head?

POMPEY
If the man be a bachelor, sir, I can; but if he be a married man, he's his wife's head, and I can never
cut off a woman's head.

If the man is a bachelor, sir, I can; but if he is Married, he is his wife's head, and I could never Cut off a woman's head.

PROVOST
Come, sir, leave me your snatches, and yield me a
direct answer. To-morrow morning are to die Claudio
and Barnardine. Here is in our prison a common executioner, who in his office lacks a helper: if you will take it on you to assist him, it shall redeem you from your gyves; if not, you shall have
your full time of imprisonment and your deliverance
with an unpitied whipping, for you have been a notorious bawd.

Come, sir, don't nitpick with me, and give me a Direct answer. Tomorrow morning Claudio And Barnadine are to die. Here, in our prison we have a common Executioner, who lacks an assistant for his position: if You will take on the task of assisting him, that will Free you from your jail time; if not, you shall have your full time of imprisonment and you will receive A remorseless whipping, for you have been a Disreputable procurer of whores.

POMPEY
Sir, I have been an unlawful bawd time out of mind;
but yet I will be content to be a lawful hangman. I
would be glad to receive some instruction from my
fellow partner.

Sir, I have procured whores against the law time and again; But I would still be happy to be a law-abiding executioner. I Would be glad to receive instructions from my New partner.

PROVOST
What, ho! Abhorson! Where's Abhorson, there?

Well then! Abhorson! Where are you, Abhorson?

Enter ABHORSON

ABHORSON
Do you call, sir?

You're calling for me, sir?

PROVOST

Sirrah, here's a fellow will help you to-morrow in
your execution. If you think it meet, compound with
him by the year, and let him abide here with you; if
not, use him for the present and dismiss him. He
cannot plead his estimation with you; he hath
been a bawd.

ABHORSON

A bawd, sir? fie upon him! he will discredit our
mystery.

PROVOST

Go to, sir; you weigh equally; a feather will turn
the scale.

POMPEY

Pray, sir, by your good favour,--for surely, sir, a
good favour you have, but that you have a hanging
look,--do you call, sir, your occupation a
mystery?

ABHORSON

Ay, sir; a mystery

POMPEY

Painting, sir, I have heard say, is a mystery; and
your whores, sir, being members of my occupation,
using painting, do prove my occupation a mystery:
but what mystery there should be in hanging, if I
should be hanged, I cannot imagine.

ABHORSON

Sir, it is a mystery.

POMPEY

Proof?

Man, here's a fellow who will help you tomorrow with
Your execution. If you think it works, settle an amount with
Him by the year, and let him live here with you; if
Not, use him for now and then dismiss him. He
Cannot plead his reputation with you; he was a whore procurer.

A procurer, sir? Bad for him! He will disgrace our craft.

Go to him, sir; you are a good judge; just a little will change Your mind.

Exit

Tell me, sir, by your good face—for surely, sir, a
Good face you have, except that you have a hanging
Look,--do you call, sir, you occupation a craft?

Yes, sir; a craft.

Cosmetics, sir, I have heard called a craft; and
Whores, sir, being associates of my kind of work,
Use cosmetics, proving my work to be a craft:
But what craft there could be in hanging people, if I
Was to be hanged, I especially could not imagine.

Sir, it is a craft.

Proof?

ABHORSON

Every true man's apparel fits your thief: if it be too little for your thief, your true man thinks it big enough; if it be too big for your thief, your thief thinks it little enough: so every true man's apparel fits your thief.

Every honest man's clothing fits a thief: if it is Too small for the thief, the honest man thinks it Is valuable enough for him; if it is too big for the thief, The thief thinks it is worthless enough for him: so every honest man's Clothing fits a thief.

Re-enter PROVOST

PROVOST

Are you agreed?

Have you come to an agreement?

POMPEY

Sir, I will serve him; for I do find your hangman is
a more penitent trade than your bawd; he doth oftener ask forgiveness.

*Sir, I will serve him; for I think that an executioner is
A more remorseful trade than a procurer of whores; he Asks for forgiveness more often.*

PROVOST

You, sirrah, provide your block and your axe to-morrow four o'clock.

You, man, bring your block and your axe Tomorrow at four o'clock.

ABHORSON

Come on, bawd; I will instruct thee in my trade; follow.

Come on, procurer; I will instruct you in my trade; follow me.

POMPEY

I do desire to learn, sir: and I hope, if you have occasion to use me for your own turn, you shall find
me yare; for truly, sir, for your kindness I owe you
a good turn.

*I do want to learn, sir: and I hope, if you have The need to use my help in hanging men, you will find
That I am ready; because honestly, sir, for your kindness I owe you
A nice favor.*

PROVOST

Call hither Barnardine and Claudio:

Call Bernardine and Claudio here:

Exeunt POMPEY and ABHORSON

The one has my pity; not a jot the other,
Being a murderer, though he were my brother.

One of them as my pity; the other one doesn't at all, Since he is a murderer, even though he was by brother.

Enter CLAUDIO

Look, here's the warrant, Claudio, for thy death:

Look Claudio, here's the warrant for your

'Tis now dead midnight, and by eight to-morrow
Thou must be made immortal. Where's
Barnardine?

CLAUDIO
As fast lock'd up in sleep as guiltless labour
When it lies starkly in the traveller's bones:
He will not wake.

PROVOST
Who can do good on him?
Well, go, prepare yourself.

But, hark, what noise?
Heaven give your spirits comfort!

By and by.
I hope it is some pardon or reprieve
For the most gentle Claudio.

Welcome father.

DUKE VINCENTIO
The best and wholesomest spirts of the night
Envelope you, good Provost! Who call'd here of
late?

PROVOST
None, since the curfew rung.

DUKE VINCENTIO
Not Isabel?

PROVOST
No.

DUKE VINCENTIO
They will, then, ere't be long.

death: It is now exactly midnight, and by eight o'clock tomorrow You must be executed. Where's Bernardine?

As dead asleep as when honest hard work Drags a workingman to rest: He will not wake up.

Who can do him any good? Well, go, prepare yourself.

Knocking within

Hey, what's that noise? May heaven give your souls a blessing!

Exit CLAUDIO

Well anyway. I hope that is a pardon or reprieve For the gentle Claudio.

Enter DUKE VINCENTIO disguised as before

Welcome father.

May the best and most wholesome spirits of the night Take you in, good Provost! Who has called here lately?

No one, since the curfew bell rang.

Not even Isabel?

No.

They will, then, before too long.

PROVOST
What comfort is for Claudio?

What reassurance is there for Claudio?

DUKE VINCENTIO
There's some in hope.

There's a little hope.

PROVOST
It is a bitter deputy.

He's such a harsh governor

DUKE VINCENTIO
Not so, not so; his life is parallel'd
Even with the stroke and line of his great
justice:
He doth with holy abstinence subdue
That in himself which he spurs on his power
To qualify in others: were he meal'd with that
Which he corrects, then were he tyrannous;
But this being so, he's just.

No he's not; he life is mirrored
Exactly with the letter of his law:
He does with heavenly self-restraint hold back
In himself the thing for which he uses his power
To punish others: if he were guilty of that
Which he punishes, then he would be a tyrant;
But as it is, he's fair.

Knocking within

Now are they come.

Now they are here.

Exit PROVOST

This is a gentle provost: seldom when
The steeled gaoler is the friend of men.

He is a kind provost: it's not often when
A hardened jailer is the friendly to others.

Knocking within

How now! what noise? That spirit's possessed
with haste
That wounds the unsisting postern with these
strokes.

What's going on! What's that noise? That
messenger is in a great hurry
Who hammers the unmoving gate with these
blows.

Re-enter PROVOST

PROVOST
There he must stay until the officer
Arise to let him in: he is call'd up.

He must stay there until an officer
Lets him in: I have called him in.

DUKE VINCENTIO
Have you no countermand for Claudio yet,
But he must die to-morrow?

Do you have a pardon for Claudio yet,
Or is he still going to die tomorrow?

PROVOST
None, sir, none.

I have none, sir.

DUKE VINCENTIO
As near the dawning, provost, as it is,
You shall hear more ere morning.

As close to sunrise as it is, provost,
You will receive one before morning.

PROVOST
Happily
You something know; yet I believe there comes
No countermand; no such example have we:
Besides, upon the very siege of justice
Lord Angelo hath to the public ear
Profess'd the contrary.

Perhaps
You know something I don't; but I believe he
will not receive a pardon; there are no examples
of that: Besides, on the very seat of justice
Lord Angelo has publicly
Announced the opposite.

Enter a Messenger

This is his lordship's man.

This is his lordship's messenger.

DUKE VINCENTIO
And here comes Claudio's pardon.

And here comes Claudio's pardon.

MESSENGER
[Giving a paper]
My lord hath sent you this note; and by me this
further charge, that you swerve not from the
smallest article of it, neither in time, matter, or
other circumstance. Good morrow; for, as I take
it,
it is almost day.

[Hands over a paper]
My lord sends you this note; and with me this
Additional instruction: to not stray from the
Smallest direction in it, not in time, or subject
matter, or Any other situation. Have a good day
tomorrow; for I believe
It's almost day.

PROVOST
I shall obey him.

I will obey him.

Exit MESSENGER

DUKE VINCENTIO
[Aside] This is his pardon, purchased by such
sin
For which the pardoner himself is in.
Hence hath offence his quick celerity,
When it is born in high authority:
When vice makes mercy, mercy's so extended,
That for the fault's love is the offender friended.
Now, sir, what news?

[Aside] This is his pardon, bought by the same
sin
That the man who pardoned him committed.
In this way, sin multiplies quickly
When it is held up by those with authority:
When sin is the reason for mercy, mercy
becomes so overstretched That for the love of
sin the prisoner is helped. Now, sir, what's the
news?

PROVOST
I told you. Lord Angelo, belike thinking me
remiss

As I told you before. Lord Angelo, perhaps
thinking I am irresponsible

in mine office, awakens me with this unwonted
putting-on; methinks strangely, for he hath not
used it before.

DUKE VINCENTIO
Pray you, let's hear.

PROVOST
[Reads]
'Whatsoever you may hear to the contrary, let
Claudio be executed by four of the clock; and in
the
afternoon Barnardine: for my better satisfaction,
let me have Claudio's head sent me by five. Let
this be duly performed; with a thought that more
depends on it than we must yet deliver. Thus fail
not to do your office, as you will answer it at
your peril.'
What say you to this, sir?

DUKE VINCENTIO
What is that Barnardine who is to be executed in
the
afternoon?

PROVOST
A Bohemian born, but here nursed up and bred;
one
that is a prisoner nine years old.

DUKE VINCENTIO
How came it that the absent duke had not either
delivered him to his liberty or executed him? I
have heard it was ever his manner to do so.

PROVOST
His friends still wrought reprieves for him: and,
indeed, his fact, till now in the government of
Lord
Angelo, came not to an undoubtful proof.

DUKE VINCENTIO
It is now apparent?

PROVOST
Most manifest, and not denied by himself.

*In my work, wakes me up with these strange
Directions; or I think it's strange, as he hasn't
done this before.*

Please, tell me what it is.

[Reads]
*'Despite whatever else you might hear,
Execute Claudio by four o'clock; and in the
Afternoon execute Barnardine: to assure me of
this Have Claudio's head sent to me by five.
This Should be properly carried out; know that
more Depends on this than I may tell you know.
So do not fail To do your job, as you will answer
for it your own risk.'
What do you think of this, sir?*

*Who is this Barnardine who is to be executed in
the
Afternoon?*

*He was born in Bohemia, but was raised here;
He has been a prisoner for the last nine years.*

*How is it that the absent duke had neither
Given him his freedom nor executed him? I
Have heard that it was his style to do so.*

*His friends were able to get a stay of execution
for him: and In fact, until now in the government
of Lord Angelo, his crime
Had not been absolutely proven.*

Is it now evident?

Most clear, not he does not deny it.

DUKE VINCENTIO
Hath he born himself penitently in prison? How
seems he to be touched?

*Has he been remorseful while in prison? How
Does he seem to be affected?*

PROVOST
A man that apprehends death no more
dreadfully but
as a drunken sleep; careless, reckless, and
fearless
of what's past, present, or to come; insensible of
mortality, and desperately mortal.

*A man that worries about death no more
fearfully than
If it were a drunken sleep; he's carless, reckless,
and fearless
Of what's in his past, present or future;
uncaring of Death, and sure to die.*

DUKE VINCENTIO
He wants advice.

He needs guidance.

PROVOST
He will hear none: he hath evermore had the
liberty
of the prison; give him leave to escape hence, he
would not: drunk many times a day, if not many
days
entirely drunk. We have very oft awaked him, as
if
to carry him to execution, and showed him a
seeming
warrant for it: it hath not moved him at all.

*He won't hear it: he has always had the freedom
To go about the prison; if you gave him a way to
escape here, he
Still wouldn't go: he's drunk most of the day,
and many days
Entirely drunk. We have often woken him up, as
if
To bring him to his execution, and showed him a
supposed
Warrant for it: it has not changed him at all.*

DUKE VINCENTIO
More of him anon. There is written in your
brow,
provost, honesty and constancy: if I read it not
truly, my ancient skill beguiles me; but, in the
boldness of my cunning, I will lay myself in
hazard.
Claudio, whom here you have warrant to
execute, is
no greater forfeit to the law than Angelo who
hath
sentenced him. To make you understand this in
a
manifested effect, I crave but four days' respite;
for the which you are to do me both a present
and a
dangerous courtesy.

*More about him in a moment. It shows on your
face,
Provost, that you are honest and consistant: if I
am in wrong In seeing that, than my practiced
skill in reading face has deceived me; but since
I am confident of my skill, I will put myself at
risk. Claudio, who's warrant of execution you
have, is
No greater criminal against the law than
Angelo, who has
Sentenced him. To make you understand this in
a
Clear way, I need only a four day delay;
In which you need to do me an immediate and
Dangerous favor.*

PROVOST
Pray, sir, in what?

Please, sir, what is it?

DUKE VINCENTIO
In the delaying death.

Delay the death.

PROVOST
A lack, how may I do it, having the hour limited,
and an express command, under penalty, to deliver
his head in the view of Angelo? I may make my case
as Claudio's, to cross this in the smallest.

How can I do that with this specific time,
And an express order, under penalty, to deliver
His head for Angelo to see? I may be sentenced to death
Like Claudio, if I don't do this exactly.

DUKE VINCENTIO
By the vow of mine order I warrant you, if my instructions may be your guide. Let this Barnardine
be this morning exccutcd, and his head born to Angelo.

By the vows I took in the holy order I guarantee
your saftey, if you Follow my instructions. Have Bernardine
Executed this morning, and send his head to Angelo.

PROVOST
Angelo hath seen them both, and will discover the favour.

Angelo has seen them both, and will discover the exchange

DUKE VINCENTIO
O, death's a great disguiser; and you may add to it.
Shave the head, and tie the beard; and say it was the desire of the penitent to be so bared before his
death: you know the course is common. If any thing
fall to you upon this, more than thanks and good fortune, by the saint whom I profess, I will plead against it with my life.

Oh but, death is a great camouflage; and you can add to it.
Shave his head, and tie up his beard; tell him it was The wish of the remorseful man to be displayed as such before his
Death: you know the practice is common. If anything
Happens to you because of this, besides thanks and good Fortune, by the saint whom I am devoted to, I will plead Against it with my life.

PROVOST
Pardon me, good father; it is against my oath.

I'm sorry, good father; but it is against my oaths.

DUKE VINCENTIO
Were you sworn to the duke, or to the deputy?

Were your oaths sworn to the duke, or to the governor?

PROVOST
To him, and to his substitutes.

To the duke and his those who take his place.

DUKE VINCENTIO

You will think you have made no offence, if the duke
avouch the justice of your dealing?

PROVOST

But what likelihood is in that?

DUKE VINCENTIO

Not a resemblance, but a certainty. Yet since I see
you fearful, that neither my coat, integrity, nor
persuasion can with ease attempt you, I will go
further than I meant, to pluck all fears out of you.
Look you, sir, here is the hand and seal of the
duke: you know the character, I doubt not; and the
signet is not strange to you.

PROVOST

I know them both.

DUKE VINCENTIO

The contents of this is the return of the duke: you
shall anon over-read it at your pleasure; where you
shall find, within these two days he will be here.
This is a thing that Angelo knows not; for he this
very day receives letters of strange tenor;
perchance of the duke's death; perchance entering
into some monastery; but, by chance, nothing of what
is writ. Look, the unfolding star calls up the
shepherd. Put not yourself into amazement how these
things should be: all difficulties are but easy
when they are known. Call your executioner, and off
with Barnardine's head: I will give him a present
shrift and advise him for a better place. Yet you
are amazed; but this shall absolutely resolve

Will you think you done nothing wrong, if the duke
Vouches for the justice of your effort?

But how likely is that?

Not even likely, but certain. But since I can tell
You are afraid, that neither my holy robes, nor integrity, nor
Persuasion can easily persuade you, I will show you More than I wanted, to take away all your fear.
Look, sir, here is the handwriting and seal of the Duke: you know the look of it, I don't doubt; and the
Seal of authority is not unfamiliar to you.

I know them both.

The meaning of this that the duke will return: you
Can later read this over at your leisure; and it will
Tell you that within the next two day he will be here This is something that Angelo doesn't know, for
Today he will receive letters with strange subjects; Perhaps the death of the duke; perhaps him entering
Into a monastery; but, as it happens, nothing of what
Is written is true. Look, the morning start calls to the Sheperd to release his sheep. Don't be amazed at how these
Things all happen: all difficulties are only easy When they are known. Call your executioner, and cut off
Bernardine's head: I will immediately go to receive his His confession and guide him to a better place. Still, you Are amazed; but this will

you.
Come away; it is almost clear dawn.

absolutely make up your mind.
Come along; it is almost dawn.

Exeunt

SCENE III. Another room in the same.

Enter POMPEY

POMPEY
I am as well acquainted here as I was in our house
of profession: one would think it were Mistress Overdone's own house, for here be many of her old
customers. First, here's young Master Rash; he's in
for a commodity of brown paper and old ginger, ninescore and seventeen pounds; of which he made
five marks, ready money: marry, then ginger was not
much in request, for the old women were all dead.
Then is there here one Master Caper, at the suit of
Master Three-pile the mercer, for some four suits of
peach-coloured satin, which now peaches him a beggar. Then have we here young Dizy, and young
Master Deep-vow, and Master Copperspur, and Master
Starve-lackey the rapier and dagger man, and young
Drop-heir that killed lusty Pudding, and Master Forthlight the tilter, and brave Master Shooty the
great traveller, and wild Half-can that stabbed Pots, and, I think, forty more; all great doers in our trade, and are now 'for the Lord's sake.'

I am as familiar here as I was in the brothel house
I worked in: you would think it was Mistress Overdone's own house, for many of her old Customers are here. First, here's young Mister Rash; he's in here
For a worthless store of brown wraping paper and old ginger,
He bought for a hundred and ninety-seven pounds; from which he only made
Three pounds and thirty-three pence, putting him in debt: remember, then ginger wasn't
In high demand, because all the old women had died.
Then there is Mister Caper here, who has a lawsuit against him from
Mister Three-pile the fabrics seller, for about four suits made of
Peach-colored satin, which now have made him a Beggar. Then we have young Dizy here, and young
Mister Deep-vow, and Mister Copperspur, and Mister
Starve-lackey the sword and dagger man, and young
Drop-heir that killed that fat heir named Pudding, and Mister Forthlight the fighter, and well dressed Mister Shoe-tie the
Great traveler, and wild Half-can here stabbed the man Pots, and, I believe, forty others; all great vistors Of our brothel, and now prisoners crying 'for Lord's sake.'

Enter ABHORSON

ABHORSON
Sirrah, bring Barnardine hither.

Man, bring Bernardine here.

BARNARDINE
[Within] A pox o' your throats! Who makes that noise there? What are you?

[Inside] I hope you get a sickness in your throat! Who is making all that Noise? Who are

you?

POMPEY

Your friends, sir; the hangman. You must be so good, sir, to rise and be put to death.

We're your friends, sir; the executioners. I you would Please, sir, wake up and be put to death.

BARNARDINE

[Within] Away, you rogue, away! I am sleepy.

[Inside] go away, you scoundrel, go away! I am sleepy.

ABHORSON

Tell him he must awake, and that quickly too.

Tell him he must wake up right away.

POMPEY

Pray, Master Barnardine, awake till you are executed, and sleep afterwards.

Please, Master Bardardine, wake up until you are Executed, and then you can sleep afterwards.

ABHORSON

Go in to him, and fetch him out.

Go in there and drag him out.

POMPEY

He is coming, sir, he is coming; I hear his straw rustle.

He's coming, sir, he's coming; I hear his bed moving.

ABHORSON

Is the axe upon the block, sirrah?

Is the axe on the execution block, man?

POMPEY

Very ready, sir.

It's ready, sir.

Enter BARNARDINE

BARNARDINE

How now, Abhorson? what's the news with you?

What now, Abhorson? What's going on with you?

ABHORSON

Truly, sir, I would desire you to clap into your prayers; for, look you, the warrant's come.

Honestly, sir, I want you to get on with your Prayers; because, look, your warrant has finally come.

BARNARDINE

You rogue, I have been drinking all night; I am not
fitted for 't.

*You scoundrel, I've been drinking all night; I'm not
Ready for it.*

POMPEY

O, the better, sir; for he that drinks all night, and is hanged betimes in the morning, may sleep the

Oh, all the better, sir; since he drank all night, And is to be hanged early in the morning, he may sleep

sounder all the next day.

ABHORSON
Look you, sir; here comes your ghostly father:
do
we jest now, think you?

DUKE VINCENTIO
Sir, induced by my charity, and hearing how
hastily
you are to depart, I am come to advise you,
comfort
you and pray with you.

BARNARDINE
Friar, not I I have been drinking hard all night,
and I will have more time to prepare me, or they
shall beat out my brains with billets: I will not
consent to die this day, that's certain.

DUKE VINCENTIO
O, sir, you must: and therefore I beseech you
Look forward on the journey you shall go.

BARNARDINE
I swear I will not die to-day for any man's
persuasion.

DUKE VINCENTIO
But hear you.

BARNARDINE
Not a word: if you have any thing to say to me,
come to my ward; for thence will not I to-day.

DUKE VINCENTIO
Unfit to live or die: O gravel heart!
After him, fellows; bring him to the block.

Soundly all the next day.

Look, sir; here comes your holy confessor: do
You still think we're joking?

Enter DUKE VINCENTIO disguised as before

Sir, encouraged by my kindness, and hearing
how quickly
You are to leave for the grave, I have come to
give you guidance and comfort
And to pray with you.

Friar, not me: I have been heavily drinking all
night, And I will have more time to prepare
myself for death, or they Will come beat out my
brains with wooden bats: I will not Agree to die
today, that's for sure.

Oh, sir, but you must: and so I beg you
To think about the journey you are about to go
on.

I swear to you I won't die today no matter who
Tries to persuade me.

But listen.

I won't listen to a word: if you have anything to
say to me, Come to my cell; because I won't be
leaving there today.

Exit

He's unfit to live or die: Oh hardened heart!
Go after him, men; bring him to the
executioners block.

Exeunt ABHORSON and POMPEY

Re-enter PROVOST

PROVOST
Now, sir, how do you find the prisoner?

Now, sir, what did you think of the prisoner?

DUKE VINCENTIO
A creature unprepared, unmeet for death;
And to transport him in the mind he is
Were damnable.

A man unprepared, and unfit for death;
And to take him away in the state of mind he is
in Is sinful.

PROVOST
Here in the prison, father,
There died this morning of a cruel fever
One Ragozine, a most notorious pirate,
A man of Claudio's years; his beard and head
Just of his colour. What if we do omit
This reprobate till he were well inclined;
And satisfy the deputy with the visage
Of Ragozine, more like to Claudio?

Here in this prison, father,
Someone died this morning of a cruel fever
he was named Ragozine, a famous pirate
About Claudio's age; his heard and hair are
The same color as Claudio's. What if we forget
about This drunk prisoner until he is better
prepared; And satisfy Angelo with the head
Of Ragozine, which looks more like Claudio?

DUKE VINCENTIO
O, 'tis an accident that heaven provides!
Dispatch it presently; the hour draws on
Prefix'd by Angelo: see this be done,
And sent according to command; whiles I
Persuade this rude wretch willingly to die.

Oh, this is a accidental coincidence given by
heaven! Sent it immediately; it is almost the time
That Angelo specified: make sure this is done,
And sent to him according to his command while
I Convince this rude villain to die willingly.

PROVOST
This shall be done, good father, presently.
But Barnardine must die this afternoon:
And how shall we continue Claudio,
To save me from the danger that might come
If he were known alive?

I will get this done immediately, good father.
But Barnardine must die this afternoon:
And how will we keep Claudio,
To save me from the danger that might come
If it were found out that he is alive?

DUKE VINCENTIO
Let this be done.
Put them in secret holds, both Barnardine and
Claudio:
Ere twice the sun hath made his journal greeting
To the under generation, you shall find
Your safety manifested.

Do this:
Put them in secret cell, both Barnardine and
Caludio:
Before the sun shines for two days over
The people outside the prison, your safety
Will become obvious.

PROVOST
I am your free dependant.

I am your willing servant.

DUKE VINCENTIO
Quick, dispatch, and send the head to Angelo.

Quick, leave, and send the head to Angelo.

Now will I write letters to Angelo,--
The provost, he shall bear them, whose contents
Shall witness to him I am near at home,
And that, by great injunctions, I am bound
To enter publicly: him I'll desire
To meet me at the consecrated fount
A league below the city; and from thence,
By cold gradation and well-balanced form,
We shall proceed with Angelo.

PROVOST
Here is the head; I'll carry it myself.

DUKE VINCENTIO
Convenient is it. Make a swift return;
For I would commune with you of such things
That want no ear but yours.

PROVOST
I'll make all speed.

ISABELLA
[Within] Peace, ho, be here!

DUKE VINCENTIO
The tongue of Isabel. She's come to know
If yet her brother's pardon be come hither:
But I will keep her ignorant of her good,
To make her heavenly comforts of despair,
When it is least expected.

ISABELLA
Ho, by your leave!

DUKE VINCENTIO
Good morning to you, fair and gracious
daughter.

ISABELLA
The better, given me by so holy a man.

Exit PROVOST

Now I will write letters to Angelo,--
The provost will take them to him, the letters
will Make him aware that I am close to home
And that, due to strict commands, I am ordered
To enter publicly: I'll want him
To meet me at the holy springs
Three miles away from the city; and from there,
With deliberate steps and careful procedures,
I will move along with Angelo.

Re-enter PROVOST

Here is the head; I'll bring it to him myself.

That's convenient. Return quickly;
Because I would like to discuss with you about
things That I need to speak about only to you.

I'll hurry.

Exit

[Inside] Peace and hello to whoever is here!

That's Isabel's voice. She's come to know
If her brother's pardon is here yet:
But I won't tell her of the good news,
In order to bring her heavenly reassurance out
of despair When she least expects it.

Enter ISABELLA

Hello, if you'll allow me in!

Good morning to you, fair and gracious
daughter.

It's better now that I have been greeted like so

Hath yet the deputy sent my brother's pardon?

by a holy man. Has the governor sent my brother's pardon yet?

DUKE VINCENTIO
He hath released him, Isabel, from the world:
His head is off and sent to Angelo.

*He has sent him away from this world, Isabel:
His head was cut off and sent to Angelo.*

ISABELLA
Nay, but it is not so.

No, but this can't be.

DUKE VINCENTIO
It is no other: show your wisdom, daughter,
In your close patience.

*That's how it is: that you are wise, daughter,
By displaying your deep patience.*

ISABELLA
O, I will to him and pluck out his eyes!

Oh, I will got to him and stab out his eyes!

DUKE VINCENTIO
You shall not be admitted to his sight.

He will not let you see him.

ISABELLA
Unhappy Claudio! wretched Isabel!
Injurious world! most damned Angelo!

*Unhappy Claudio! Miserable Isabel!
Unfair world! And most of all damn you Angelo!*

DUKE VINCENTIO
This nor hurts him nor profits you a jot;
Forbear it therefore; give your cause to heaven.
Mark what I say, which you shall find
By every syllable a faithful verity:
The duke comes home to-morrow; nay, dry your eyes;
One of our convent, and his confessor,
Gives me this instance: already he hath carried
Notice to Escalus and Angelo,
Who do prepare to meet him at the gates,
There to give up their power. If you can, pace your wisdom
In that good path that I would wish it go,
And you shall have your bosom on this wretch,
Grace of the duke, revenges to your heart,
And general honour.

*This neither hurts him nor benefits you at all;
So restrain yourself; give up your reaction.
Listen to what I say, as you will find
Every syllable to be very true:
The duke comes home tomorrow; no, don't cry;
Someone from out holy order, and his confessor,
Told me of this: he has already sent
Notes to Escalus and Angelo,
Who are preparing to meet him at the gates,
And to give up their authority. If you can,
control your thoughts
In the right way that I want,
And you shall have your heart's desire inflicted
on this scoundrel
By the honor of the duke, revenge to your
heart's content, And general honor.*

ISABELLA
I am directed by you.

I am listening to your instructions.

DUKE VINCENTIO
This letter, then, to Friar Peter give;

Then, give this letter to Friar Peter;

'Tis that he sent me of the duke's return:
Say, by this token, I desire his company
At Mariana's house to-night. Her cause and yours
I'll perfect him withal, and he shall bring you
Before the duke, and to the head of Angelo
Accuse him home and home. For my poor self,
I am combined by a sacred vow
And shall be absent. Wend you with this letter:
Command these fretting waters from your eyes
With a light heart; trust not my holy order,
If I pervert your course. Who's here?

He's the one that told me of the duke's return:
Tell him, with this as proof, that I would like to
see him At Mariana's house tonight. I'll tell him
about your
And Mariana's situations, and he will bring you
Before the duke, and to Angelo's face
Accuse him thoroughly. For my poor self,
I am tied up by sacred vow
And won't be there. Go with this letter:
Order those tears to leave your eyes
With a little happiness; don't trust my holy
order, If I steer your wrong. Who's there?

Enter LUCIO

LUCIO
Good even. Friar, where's the provost?

Good evening. Friar, where's the provost?

DUKE VINCETNTIO
Not within, sir.

Not here, sir.

LUCIO
O pretty Isabella, I am pale at mine heart to see
thine eyes so red: thou must be patient. I am fain
to dine and sup with water and bran; I dare not for
my head fill my belly; one fruitful meal would set
me to 't. But they say the duke will be here
to-morrow. By my troth, Isabel, I loved thy brother:
if the old fantastical duke of dark corners had been
at home, he had lived.

Oh pretty Isabella, I am sick at heart to see
Your eyes so red: you must be patient. I must
Eat dinner and supper with water and brown
bread; I can't
Fill my belly for fear of going crazy; one filling
meal would
Send me over the edge. But they say the duke
will be here Tomorrow. Honestly, Isabel, I
loved your brother:
If the old quirky duke with hidden secrets had
been
Home, your brother would have lived.

Exit ISABELLA

DUKE VINCENTIO
Sir, the duke is marvellous little beholding to your
reports; but the best is, he lives not in them.

Sir, the duke owes you very little favor for
Your information about him; but the good thing
is, he is not like you say.

LUCIO
Friar, thou knowest not the duke so well as I do:
he's a better woodman than thou takest him for.

Friar, you don't know the duke as well as I do:
He's a better woman hunter than you take him
for.

DUKE VINCENTIO

Well, you'll answer this one day. Fare ye well.

LUCIO
Nay, tarry; I'll go along with thee
I can tell thee pretty tales of the duke.

DUKE VINCENTIO
You have told me too many of him already, sir, if
they be true; if not true, none were enough.

LUCIO
I was once before him for getting a wench with child.

DUKE VINCENTIO
Did you such a thing?

LUCIO
Yes, marry, did I but I was fain to forswear it;
they would else have married me to the rotten medlar.

DUKE VINCENTIO
Sir, your company is fairer than honest. Rest you well.

LUCIO
By my troth, I'll go with thee to the lane's end:
if bawdy talk offend you, we'll have very little of
it. Nay, friar, I am a kind of burr; I shall stick.

Well, you'll be held accountable for this one day. Good bye.

*No, wait; I'll go with you
I can tell you witty stories about the duke.*

*You have told me too many stories about him already, sir, if
They're true; if they're not true, than no stories were enough.*

I was once judged by him for getting a woman pregnant.

You did such a thing?

Yes, by holy Virgin Mary, I did but I was ready to deny it Otherwise it would have ruined my reputation with the whores.

Sir, you company is more entertaining than it is truthful. Have a good day.

*Honestly, I'll go with you to the end of the road:
If crass talk offends you, we won't speak that Way. No, friar, I am like a burr; I will stick to you.*

Exeunt

SCENE IV. A room in ANGELO's house.

ESCALUS
Every letter he hath writ hath disvouched other.

Every letter he has written has discredited another.

ANGELO
In most uneven and distracted manner. His actions
show much like to madness: pray heaven his wisdom be
not tainted! And why meet him at the gates, and redeliver our authorities there

In a very odd and distracter manner. His actions Are similar to madness: pray to heaven that his intellect isn't Spoiled! And why do we have to meet him at the gates, and Surrender our authority there?

ESCALUS
I guess not.

I don't know.

ANGELO
And why should we proclaim it in an hour before his
entering, that if any crave redress of injustice, they should exhibit their petitions in the street?

And why should be announce an hour before his Arrival, that if there was any need to put injustice to rights, That they should declare their complaints in the street?

ESCALUS
He shows his reason for that: to have a dispatch of
complaints, and to deliver us from devices hereafter, which shall then have no power to stand
against us.

He says the reason for that: to quickly settle all Complaints, and to save us from fake complaints After this, which won't have the ability to be held Against us.

ANGELO
Well, I beseech you, let it be proclaimed betimes i' the morn; I'll call you at your house: give notice to such men of sort and suit as are to meet him.

Well, I ask you, why not announce it early In the morning; I'll stop by to visit you at your house: let The men of proper social status and outfit know they are going to meet Him.

ESCALUS
I shall, sir. Fare you well.

I will, sir. Good bye.

ANGELO
Good night.

Good night.

116

This deed unshapes me quite, makes me unpregnant
And dull to all proceedings. A deflower'd maid!
And by an eminent body that enforced
The law against it! But that her tender shame
Will not proclaim against her maiden loss,
How might she tongue me! Yet reason dares her no;
For my authority bears of a credent bulk,
That no particular scandal once can touch
But it confounds the breather. He should have lived,
Save that riotous youth, with dangerous sense,
Might in the times to come have ta'en revenge,
By so receiving a dishonour'd life
With ransom of such shame. Would yet he had lived!
A lack, when once our grace we have forgot,
Nothing goes right: we would, and we would not.

This act quite confuses me, and makes me unprepared
And slow to react to all these events. A lady's virginity lost! And taken by an important man that enforced The law against such things! Were it not that because of her unfortunate shame She cannot publically speak out against her loss of virginity, Think of how she would accuse me! But reason frightens her away from it; Because my authority has such strong credibility, There is not a single scandal that can stain it Unless it harms the one complaining of it as well. He could have lived, Except that rebellious youngster, with dangerous knowledge of this, Might have later come to take his revenge, For being given a dishonorable life Bought with such shame. Still I wish he had lived!
Oh well, once we have forgotten our virtue, Nothing is right: we could do one thing as easily as another.

Exit

SCENE V. Fields without the town.

Enter DUKE VINCENTIO in his own habit, and FRIAR PETER

DUKE VINCENTIO

These letters at fit time deliver me

Deliver these letters at the right time for me.

Giving letters

The provost knows our purpose and our plot.
The matter being afoot, keep your instruction,
And hold you ever to our special drift;
Though sometimes you do blench from this to that,
As cause doth minister. Go call at Flavius' house,
And tell him where I stay: give the like notice
To Valentinus, Rowland, and to Crassus,
And bid them bring the trumpets to the gate;
But send me Flavius first.

*The provost knows our situation and our plan.
That task being at hand, stick to your duty,
And remember our precise purpose,
Though you may sometimes vary from this to that
As necessity requires. Go visit at Flavius' house,
And tell him where I am staying: say the same thing To Valentinus, Rowland, and to Crassus
And ask them to bring trumpeters to the gate;
But tell Flavius first.*

FRIAR PETER

It shall be speeded well.

I will do it quickly.

Exit

Enter VARRIUS

DUKE VINCENTIO

I thank thee, Varrius; thou hast made good haste:
Come, we will walk. There's other of our friends
Will greet us here anon, my gentle Varrius.

*Thank you, Varrius; you have hurried here in time:
Come on, let's take a walk. More of our friends
Will join us in a moment, my good man Varrius.*

Exeunt

SCENE VI. Street near the city gate.

ISABELLA
To speak so indirectly I am loath:
I would say the truth; but to accuse him so,
That is your part: yet I am advised to do it;
He says, to veil full purpose.

*I hate to speak so dishonestly:
I want to say the trith; but accusing him
truthfully Is your job: but I have been told to do
it; He says to hide the true reason.*

MARIANA
Be ruled by him.

Listen to him.

ISABELLA
Besides, he tells me that, if peradventure
He speak against me on the adverse side,
I should not think it strange; for 'tis a physic
That's bitter to sweet end.

*Besides, he says that, if by chance
He were to speak against me of the opposing
side, I shouldn't think it's strange; because it's
a solution That's difficult but for a good result.*

MARIANA
I would Friar Peter—

I wish Friar Peter--

ISABELLA
O, peace! the friar is come.

Oh good! The friar is here.

Enter FRIAR PETER

FRIAR PETER
Come, I have found you out a stand most fit,
Where you may have such vantage on the duke,
He shall not pass you. Twice have the trumpets
sounded;
The generous and gravest citizens
Have hent the gates, and very near upon
The duke is entering: therefore, hence, away!

*Come here, I have found you a good place to
stand, Where you may see the duke well enough,
That he cannot pass you. The trumpets have
sounded twice;
The kind and serious citizens
Have arrived at the gates, and very soon
The duke will enter: so go there, away with you!*

Exeunt

ACT V

SCENE I. The city gate.

MARIANA veiled, ISABELLA, and FRIAR PETER, at their stand. Enter DUKE VINCENTIO, VARRIUS, Lords, ANGELO, ESCALUS, LUCIO, PROVOST, Officers, and Citizens, at several doors

DUKE VINCENTIO
My very worthy cousin, fairly met!
Our old and faithful friend, we are glad to see you.

*My wonderful friend, nice to see you!
And our old and faithful friend, I'm glad to see you too.*

ANGELO ESCALUS
Happy return be to your royal grace!

Welcome home, your royal grace!

DUKE VINCENTIO
Many and hearty thankings to you both.
We have made inquiry of you; and we hear
Such goodness of your justice, that our soul
Cannot but yield you forth to public thanks,
Forerunning more requital.

*Thank you both so much.
We've asked about your work; and we've heard
Such good things of your justice, that we
Cannot help but it thank you publicly,
Before showing you more gratitude.*

ANGELO
You make my bonds still greater.

You continue to make me indebted to you.

DUKE VINCENTIO
O, your desert speaks loud; and I should wrong it,
To lock it in the wards of covert bosom,
When it deserves, with characters of brass,
A forted residence 'gainst the tooth of time
And razure of oblivion. Give me your hand,
And let the subject see, to make them know
That outward courtesies would fain proclaim
Favours that keep within. Come, Escalus,
You must walk by us on our other hand;
And good supporters are you.

*Oh, your praiseworthiness is great; and I would do you wrong,
To keep it locked up in my heart,
When it deserves, with brass plaques,
A castle against the ravages if time
And obliteration into oblivion. Give me your hand, And let the people of the city see, to make sure they know That outward displays of courtesy would happily show The high regard we hold inside our hearts. Come on, Escalus, You must walk on my other side; You're such good followers.*

FRIAR PETER and ISABELLA come forward

FRIAR PETER
Now is your time: speak loud and kneel before him.

Now it's time: speak loudly and kneel in front of him

ISABELLA
Justice, O royal duke! Vail your regard

Justice, oh royal duke! Look down

FRIAR PETER
Now is your time: speak loud and kneel before him.

Now it's time: speak loudly and kneel in front of him.

ISABELLA
Justice, O royal duke! Vail your regard
Upon a wrong'd, I would fain have said, a maid!
O worthy prince, dishonour not your eye
By throwing it on any other object
Till you have heard me in my true complaint
And given me justice, justice, justice, justice!

Justice, oh royal duke! Look down On someone who has been wronged, I would gladly have once called myself a virgin! Oh worthy duke, don't spoil your eyes By looking at any one else Until you have heard my whole complaint And have given my justice, justice, justice, justice!

DUKE VINCENTIO
Relate your wrongs; in what? by whom? be brief.
Here is Lord Angelo shall give you justice:
Reveal yourself to him.

*Explain how you were wronged; how so? And by whom? Tell me quickly.
Here is Lord Angelo to give you justice: Explain yourself to him.*

ISABELLA
O worthy duke,
You bid me seek redemption of the devil:
Hear me yourself; for that which I must speak
Must either punish me, not being believed,
Or wring redress from you. Hear me, O hear me, here!

*Oh, worthy duke,
You are asking me to seek retribution from an evil man: Listen to me yourself; for what I am about to tell you will either punish me, if you don't believe me, Or force you to provide compensation for my wrongs. Listen to me, oh listen to me, right now!*

ANGELO
My lord, her wits, I fear me, are not firm:
She hath been a suitor to me for her brother
Cut off by course of justice,--

My lord, I'm afraid her mind is not sound: She has been begging me to free her brother Executed in accordance with the law,--

ISABELLA
By course of justice!

In accordance with the law!

ANGELO
And she will speak most bitterly and strange.

And what she has to say will be angry and strange.

ISABELLA
Most strange, but yet most truly, will I speak:
That Angelo's forsworn; is it not strange?
That Angelo's a murderer; is 't not strange?
That Angelo is an adulterous thief,

What I have to say is quite strange, but still it is true: Is it not strange that Angelo would be a liar? Is it not strange that Angelo would be a murderer? That Angelo is a two-timing thief,

An hypocrite, a virgin-violator;
Is it not strange and strange?

*A hypocrite, and violated a virgin;
It that not all quite strange?*

DUKE VINCENTIO
Nay, it is ten times strange.

No, it is stranger than strange.

ISABELLA
It is not truer he is Angelo
Than this is all as true as it is strange:
Nay, it is ten times true; for truth is truth
To the end of reckoning.

*It's just as true the he is named Angelo
That all this is as true as it is strange:
No, it is truer than true; for truth is truth
Until the end of time.*

DUKE VINCENTIO
Away with her! Poor soul,
She speaks this in the infirmity of sense.

*Take her away! Poor woman,
She speaks all this with an insane mind.*

ISABELLA
O prince, I conjure thee, as thou believest
There is another comfort than this world,
That thou neglect me not, with that opinion
That I am touch'd with madness! Make not
impossible
That which but seems unlike: 'tis not impossible
But one, the wicked'st caitiff on the ground,
May seem as shy, as grave, as just, as absolute
As Angelo; even so may Angelo,
In all his dressings, characts, titles, forms,
Be an arch-villain; believe it, royal prince:
If he be less, he's nothing; but he's more,
Had I more name for badness.

*Oh duke, I beg of you, as you believe
That there is a heaven beyond this world,
That you not neglect me, because you think
I have gone insane! Do not say it is impossible
Because it is unlikely: it's not impossible
That the most evil scoundrel on the face of the
earth, May seem as withdrawn, as distinguished,
as honorable, and as honest As Angelo does;
just as Angelo could, With all this official robes
and badges and titles and actions, Be an arch-
villain; believe me, royal duke: If he is better
than what I am claim, than he's nothing at all;
but I would call him worse If I had more words
for evilness.*

DUKE VINCENTIO
By mine honesty,
If she be mad,--as I believe no other,--
Her madness hath the oddest frame of sense,
Such a dependency of thing on thing,
As e'er I heard in madness.

*Honestly,
If she is crazy,--and I believe that to be the
case,-- Her insanity has strange coherent logic.
I've never heard such a logical progression of
ideas From an insane person.*

ISABELLA
O gracious duke,
Harp not on that, nor do not banish reason
For inequality; but let your reason serve
To make the truth appear where it seems hid,
And hide the false seems true.

*Oh kind duke,
Don't think very long about that, and don't
assume I am not logical Because I am beneath
you in rank; but instead use your logic to
Discover that the truth only seems like an
impossible lie, And the actual lie seems to be the*

DUKE VINCENTIO
Many that are not mad
Have, sure, more lack of reason. What would
you say?

ISABELLA
I am the sister of one Claudio,
Condemn'd upon the act of fornication
To lose his head; condemn'd by Angelo:
I, in probation of a sisterhood,
Was sent to by my brother; one Lucio
As then the messenger,--

LUCIO
That's I, an't like your grace:
I came to her from Claudio, and desired her
To try her gracious fortune with Lord Angelo
For her poor brother's pardon.

ISABELLA
That's he indeed.

DUKE VINCENTIO
You were not bid to speak.

LUCIO
No, my good lord;
Nor wish'd to hold my peace.

DUKE VINCENTIO
I wish you now, then;
Pray you, take note of it: and when you have
A business for yourself, pray heaven you then
Be perfect.

LUCIO
I warrant your honour.

DUKE VINCENTIO
The warrants for yourself; take heed to't.

ISABELLA
This gentleman told somewhat of my tale,--

truth.

Many who are not crazy
Make less reasonable sense, for sure. What do
you have to say?

I am the sister of Claudio,
Who committed the sin of having sexual
relations And was sentenced to lose his head;
sentenced to this by Angelo: I was a novice at
the convent, When my brother sent for me;
Lucio Was the messenger,--

That would be me, if you want to know, your
grace: I came to speak to her for Claudio, and
wanted her To try her good luck with Lord
Angelo To get her poor brother pardoned.

That's him in fact.

You were not asked to speak.

No, my good lord;
Nor was I asked to be silent.

Well, I am asking you now, then;
Please, obey my wishes: and when you have
A problem of your own, hope that you behave
Perfectly.

I will your honor.

The warning is for you; listen to it.

This gentleman told me part of what I have to
say now,-

LUCIO
Right.

That's right.

DUKE VINCENTIO
It may be right; but you are i' the wrong
To speak before your time. Proceed.

It may be right; but you are in the wrong
To speak before you are asked to. Continue.

ISABELLA
I wen.
To this pernicious caitiff deputy,--

I went
To this evil scoundrel of a governor,--

DUKE VINCENTIO
That's somewhat madly spoken.

That was said with an insane tone.

ISABELLA
Pardon it;
The phrase is to the matter.

I'm sorry;
The phrase is appropriate

DUKE VINCENTIO
Mended again. The matter; proceed.

I forgive you again. Continue your story.

ISABELLA
In brief, to set the needless process by,
How I persuaded, how I pray'd, and kneel'd
How he refell'd me, and how I replied,--
For this was of much length,--the vile
conclusion
I now begin with grief and shame to utter:
He would not, but by gift of my chaste body
To his concupiscible intemperate lust,
Release my brother; and, after much
debatement,
My sisterly remorse confutes mine honour,
And I did yield to him: but the next morn
betimes,
His purpose surfeiting, he sends a warrant
For my poor brother's head.

In short, to leave out the unnecessary details,
Of how I begged him, and prayed, and kneeled
in front of him, And how he refused me, and how
I responded,-- For that took a long time,--I will
now tell you the terrible result Which I am sorry
and ashamed to speak of: He would not, unless I
gave my virginity Over to his heated and
uncontrollable lustful passion, Free my brother;
and, after much arguing, My holy remorse
overcame my virtue, And I gave in to him: but
early the next morning, His desire having been
accomplished, he sent out a warrant For my
poor brother's death.

DUKE VINCENTIO
This is most likely!

Well, that sounds likely!

ISABELLA
O, that it were as like as it is true!

Oh, I wish it sounded as likely is it is true!

DUKE VINCENTIO
By heaven, fond wretch, thou knowist not what

Dear God, foolish wench, you don't know what

thou speak'st,
Or else thou art suborn'd against his honour
In hateful practise. First, his integrity
Stands without blemish. Next, it imports no reason
That with such vehemency he should pursue
Faults proper to himself: if he had so offended,
He would have weigh'd thy brother by himself
And not have cut him off. Some one hath set you on:
Confess the truth, and say by whose advice
Thou camest here to complain.

ISABELLA
And is this all?
Then, O you blessed ministers above,
Keep me in patience, and with ripen'd time
Unfold the evil which is here wrapt up
In countenance! Heaven shield your grace from woe,
As I, thus wrong'd, hence unbelieved go!

DUKE VINCENTIO
I know you'ld fain be gone. An officer!
To prison with her! Shall we thus permit
A blasting and a scandalous breath to fall
On him so near us? This needs must be a practise.
Who knew of Your intent and coming hither?

ISABELLA
One that I would were here, Friar Lodowick.

DUKE VINCENTIO
A ghostly father, belike. Who knows that
Lodowick?

LUCIO
My lord, I know him; 'tis a meddling friar;
I do not like the man: had he been lay, my lord
For certain words he spake against your grace
In your retirement, I had swinged him soundly.

DUKE VINCENTIO
Words against me? this is a good friar, belike!

---

you're saying,
Or else have been bribed to ruin his honor
In a terrible conspiracy. First, his
righteousness Has never had a word said
against it. Next, makes no sense
That he would so adamantely pursue
Punishing a crime he committed: if he has
committed such a crime, He would have judged
your brother from his own example And not
have executed him. Some one has paid you to do
this: Confess the truth, and say by whose
guidance You came here to complain.

That's all?
Then, oh you blessed angels above,
Give me patience, and in good time
Reveal the evil that is now disguised
By social rank! Heaven protect your grace from
misfortune, As I, having been wronged, go on
not being believed.

I know you would gladly be gone. Officer!
Take her to prison! How could be allow
Such hurtful and scandalous talk to be directed
Towards a man so close to us? This must be a
conspiracy. Who know of your purpose in
coming here?

Someone I wish were here, Friar Lodowick.

A holy father, presumably. Who knows this
Lodowick?

My lord, I know him; he's a meddling friar;
I don't like the man: if he hadn't been a
clergyman, my lord For certain words he spoke
against your grace In your absence, I would
have punched him soundly.

Words against me? This is a good friar,

And to set on this wretched woman here
Against our substitute! Let this friar be found.

presumably! And to set this terrible woman here up Against my replacement! Find this friar.

LUCIO
But yesternight, my lord, she and that friar,
I saw them at the prison: a saucy friar,
A very scurvy fellow.

*But last night, my lord, she and that friar,
I saw them at the prison: a disrespectful friar,
A very despicable fellow.*

FRIAR PETER
Blessed be your royal grace!
I have stood by, my lord, and I have heard
Your royal ear abused. First, hath this woman
Most wrongfully accused your substitute,
Who is as free from touch or soil with her
As she from one ungot.

*Bless you, your royal grace!
I have stood aside, my lord, and I have heard
Your royal ear mislead. First, this woman has
Most wrongfully accused your substitute,
Who is as innocent these from moral accusation
from her As she is from an unborn baby.*

DUKE VINCENTIO
We did believe no less.
Know you that Friar Lodowick that she speaks
of?

*That is exactly what we thought.
Do you know that Friar Lodowick that she
speaks of?*

FRIAR PETER
I know him for a man divine and holy;
Not scurvy, nor a temporary meddler,
As he's reported by this gentleman;
And, on my trust, a man that never yet
Did, as hc vouches, misreport your grace.

*I know him as a man who is divine and holy;
Not despicable, nor a meddler in mundane
affairs, As he's claimed to be by this gentleman;
And, I promise, a man that has never,
As he claims, insult your grace.*

LUCIO
My lord, most villanously; believe it.

My lord, he did most maliciously; believe me.

FRIAR PETER
Well, he in time may come to clear himself;
But at this instant he is sick my lord,
Of a strange fever. Upon his mere request,
Being come to knowledge that there was
complaint
Intended 'gainst Lord Angelo, came I hither,
To speak, as from his mouth, what he doth know
Is true and false; and what he with his oath
And all probation will make up full clear,
Whensoever he's convented. First, for this
woman.
To justify this worthy nobleman,
So vulgarly and personally accused,

*Well, in a little while he make come to clear his
name; But at this moment he is sick my lord,
With some unknown fever. On his personal
request, Having discovered that there was a
complaint
Planned against Lord Angelo, I came here,
To speak for him, about what he knows
To be true and false; and about what he with is
holy oath And all of the proof will make
absolutely clear, Whenever he's summoned to
speak. Firstly, about this woman.
To vindicate this worthy nobleman,
So crassly and personally accused*

Her shall you hear disproved to her eyes,
Till she herself confess it.

DUKE VINCENTIO
Good friar, let's hear it.

You will hear her disproved to her eyes,
Until she confesses to it herself.

Good friar, let's hear what you have to say.

ISABELLA is carried off guarded; and
MARIANA comes forward

Do you not smile at this, Lord Angelo?
O heaven, the vanity of wretched fools!
Give us some seats. Come, cousin Angelo;
In this I'll be impartial; be you judge
Of your own cause. Is this the witness, friar?
First, let her show her face, and after speak.

Are you not smiling at this, Lord Angelo?
By God, the arrogance of worthless fools! Give
us some seats. Come on, my good friend Angelo;
In this I'll be neutral; you be the judge Of your
own problem. Is this the witness, friar? First, let
her show her face, and after that let's hear her
speak.

MARIANA
Pardon, my lord; I will not show my face
Until my husband bid me.

I'm sorry, my lord; I will not show my face
Until my husband tells me to.

DUKE VINCENTIO
What, are you married?

What, are you married?

MARIANA
No, my lord.

No, my lord.

DUKE VINCENTIO
Are you a maid?

Are you a virgin?

MARIANA
No, my lord.

No, my lord.

DUKE VINCENTIO
A widow, then?

A widow, then?

MARIANA
Neither, my lord.

Not that either, my lord.

DUKE VINCENTIO
Why, you are nothing then: neither maid,
widow, nor wife?

Well, you are nothing then if you are not a
virgin, a widow, or a wife?

LUCIO
My lord, she may be a punk; for many of them

My lord, she may be a whore; for many of them

are
neither maid, widow, nor wife.

DUKE VINCENTIO
Silence that fellow: I would he had some cause
To prattle for himself.

LUCIO
Well, my lord.

MARIANA
My lord; I do confess I ne'er was married;
And I confess besides I am no maid:
I have known my husband; yet my husband
Knows not that ever he knew me.

LUCIO
He was drunk then, my lord: it can be no better.

DUKE VINCENTIO
For the benefit of silence, would thou wert so too!

LUCIO
Well, my lord.

DUKE VINCENTIO
This is no witness for Lord Angelo.

MARIANA
Now I come to't my lord
She that accuses him of fornication,
In self-same manner doth accuse my husband,
And charges him my lord, with such a time
When I'll depose I had him in mine arms
With all the effect of love.

ANGELO
Charges she more than me?

MARIANA
Not that I know.

DUKE VINCENTIO

---

are
Neither a virgin, a window or a wife.

Silence that man: I wish he had some case
To defend for himself.

Well, my lord.

My lord; I do admit that I was never married;
And I admit as well that I am not a virgin:
I have slept with my husband; but my husband
Did not know it was me.

He was drunk then, my lord: it can't be anything
else.

To keep you quite, I wish you were drunk too!

Well, my lord.

This is not a witness for Lord Angelo's case.

Now I'm getting to the point my lord,
The woman who accuses him of having sex,
Is at the same time accusing my husband,
And accuses him, my lord, of committing the
crime at a certain time When I can prove that I
had him in mine arms Making love.

Is she accusing more men than just me?

Not that I know of.

No? you say your husband.

No? you said your husband.

MARIANA
Why, just, my lord, and that is Angelo,
Who thinks he knows that he ne'er knew my
body,
But knows he thinks that he knows Isabel's.

*Well, yes, my lord, and that is Angelo,
Who incorrectly believes that he never had sex
with me, But instead mistakenly believes that he
was with Isabel.*

ANGELO
This is a strange abuse. Let's see thy face.

*This is a strange accusation. Let us see your
face.*

MARIANA
My husband bids me; now I will unmask.

*My husband has asked me; now I will show my
face.*

Unveiling

This is that face, thou cruel Angelo,
Which once thou sworest was worth the looking
on;
This is the hand which, with a vow'd contract,
Was fast belock'd in thine; this is the body
That took away the match from Isabel,
And did supply thee at thy garden-house
In her imagined person.

*This is the face, you cruel man Angelo,
That you once swore was worth looking at;
This is the hand that, with a promise of
marriage,
Was locked steadfastly with yours; this is the
body That during that tryst stood in place of
Isabel, And fulfilled your desire at your garden-
house Pretending to be her.*

DUKE VINCENTIO
Know you this woman?

Do you know this woman?

LUCIO
Carnally, she says.

Sexually, she claims.

DUKE VINCENTIO
Sirrah, no more!

Man, don't speak!

LUCIO
Enough, my lord.

Enough, my lord.

ANGELO
My lord, I must confess I know this woman:
And five years since there was some speech of
marriage
Betwixt myself and her; which was broke off,
Partly for that her promised proportions

*My lord, I must admit that I do know this
woman: And five years ago there was talk of
marriage
Between myself and her; which was broken off,
Partly because her promised dowry*

Came short of composition, but in chief
For that her reputation was disvalued
In levity: since which time of five years
I never spake with her, saw her, nor heard from her,
Upon my faith and honour.

Was less than was promised, but primarily
Because her reputation was discredited
Because of sexual impurity: since that time five
years agoI have never spoken with her, saw her,
or heard from her
I swear on my loyalty and honor.

MARIANA
Noble prince,
As there comes light from heaven and words from breath,
As there is sense in truth and truth in virtue,
I am affianced this man's wife as strongly
As words could make up vows: and, my good lord,
But Tuesday night last gone in's garden-house
He knew me as a wife. As this is true,
Let me in safety raise me from my knees
Or else for ever be confixed here,
A marble monument!

Noble duke,
Just as light comes from the sky and words come
from our mouths,
Just as there is reasonableness in truth and
honesty in virtue, I was engaged to be this man's
wife as certainly As words are part of vows:
and, my good lord,
Just last Tuesday night in his garden-house
He made love to me as his wife. And this is the
truth, Let me stand up from kneeling
Or else forever be fixed in this spot
Like a marble statue!

ANGELO
I did but smile till now:
Now, good my lord, give me the scope of justice
My patience here is touch'd. I do perceive
These poor informal women are no more
But instruments of some more mightier member
That sets them on: let me have way, my lord,
To find this practise out.

I only smiled at these silly accusations until
now: Now, my good lord, allow me the power of
justice My patience is growing thin, I believe
These poor crazy women are no more
Than tools of some greater member
Of the plot that put them up to this: let me have
the right, my lord, To uncover this conspiracy.

DUKE VINCENTIO
Ay, with my heart
And punish them to your height of pleasure.
Thou foolish friar, and thou pernicious woman,
Compact with her that's gone, think'st thou thy oaths,
Though they would swear down each particular saint,
Were testimonies against his worth and credit
That's seal'd in approbation? You, Lord Escalus,
Sit with my cousin; lend him your kind pains
To find out this abuse, whence 'tis derived.
There is another friar that set them on;
Let him be sent for.

Yes, whole heartedly,
And punish them as much as you want.
That foolish friar, and this malicious woman,
Conspiring with the one who was taken away,
think about your oaths,
Even though they would swear to each and
every saint,
That they were testimonies against your
significance and credibility As exact evidence?
You, Lord Escalus, Sit with my good friend; lend
him a hand In discovering these allegations, and
where they originated. There is this other friar
that set them up to this; Send for him.

FRIAR PETER

Would he were here, my lord! for he indeed
Hath set the women on to this complaint:
Your provost knows the place where he abides
And he may fetch him.

DUKE VINCENTIO
Go do it instantly.

I wish her were here, my lord! Because he did indeed Put these women up to this complaint: Your provost knows the place where he lives And he can go get him.

Go do it right this minute.

Exit PROVOST

And you, my noble and well-warranted cousin,
Whom it concerns to hear this matter forth,
Do with your injuries as seems you best,
In any chastisement: I for a while will leave
you;
But stir not you till you have well determined
Upon these slanderers.

ESCALUS
My lord, we'll do it throughly.

And you, my noble and much-admired friend, As it concerns you to hear this situation fully, Deal with your accusations as you see fit, With any punishment: I will leave you for a while; But don't move until you have passed judgment On these slanderers.

My lord, we will punish them thoroughly.

Exit DUKE

Signior Lucio, did not you say you knew that
Friar Lodowick to be a dishonest person?

Mister Lucio, didn't you say that you knew that Friar Lodowick was a dishonest person?

LUCIO
'Cucullus non facit monachum:' honest in
nothing
but in his clothes; and one that hath spoke most
villanous speeches of the duke.

'The robes don't make the monk:' nothing is honest about him Except his clothes; and he has spoken most Malicious words about the duke.

ESCALUS
We shall entreat you to abide here till he come
and
enforce them against him: we shall find this friar
a notable fellow.

We ask you to stay here until he comes and Accuse him of his words: we will find this friar to be a Noteworthy fellow.

LUCIO
As any in Vienna, on my word.

As notable as any in Vienna, I promise.

ESCALUS
Call that same Isabel here once again; I would
speak with her.

Call that woman Isabel back here; I would like to speak to here.

Exit an Attendant

Pray you, my lord, give me leave to question; you
shall see how I'll handle her.

Please, my lord, allow me to question her; you
Will she how I'll deal with her.

LUCIO
Not better than he, by her own report.

No better than he did, as she claims.

ESCALUS
Say you?

What are you saying?

LUCIO
Marry, sir, I think, if you handled her privately,
she would sooner confess: perchance, publicly,
she'll be ashamed.

By the Holy Virgin, sir, I think if you handled
her privately, She'd be more likely to confess:
perhaps, publicly, She'll be too ashamed.

ESCALUS
I will go darkly to work with her.

I well question her crypticly.

LUCIO
That's the way; for women are light at midnight.

That's how to do it; women are more willing in
the dark.

Re-enter Officers with ISABELLA; and
PROVOST with the DUKE VINCENTIO in his
friar's habit

ESCALUS
Come on, mistress: here's a gentlewoman denies all
that you have said.

Come here, mistress: there's a lady here who
denies all
That you have said.

LUCIO
My lord, here comes the rascal I spoke of; here
with
the provost.

My lord, here comes the scoundrel I mentioned;
here with
The provost.

ESCALUS
In very good time: speak not you to him till we
call upon you.

Just in time: don't speak to him until we
Ask you to.

LUCIO
Mum.

Not a word.

ESCALUS
Come, sir: did you set these women on to

Tell me, sir: did you put these women up to

slander
Lord Angelo? they have confessed you did.

DUKE VINCENTIO
'Tis false.

ESCALUS
How! know you where you are?

DUKE VINCENTIO
Respect to your great place! and let the devil
Be sometime honour'd for his burning throne!
Where is the duke? 'tis he should hear me speak.

ESCALUS
The duke's in us; and we will hear you speak:
Look you speak justly.

DUKE VINCENTIO
Boldly, at least. But, O, poor souls,
Come you to seek the lamb here of the fox?
Good night to your redress! Is the duke gone?
Then is your cause gone too. The duke's unjust,
Thus to retort your manifest appeal,
And put your trial in the villain's mouth
Which here you come to accuse.

LUCIO
This is the rascal; this is he I spoke of.

ESCALUS
Why, thou unreverend and unhallow'd friar,
Is't not enough thou hast suborn'd these women
To accuse this worthy man, but, in foul mouth
And in the witness of his proper ear,
To call him villain? and then to glance from him
To the duke himself, to tax him with injustice?
Take him hence; to the rack with him! We'll touse you
Joint by joint, but we will know his purpose.
What 'unjust'!

slander
Lord Aneglo? They confessed that you did.

That's not true.

What's this! Do you know where you are?

I respect your great place! And the devil is Sometimes honored for being the king of hell! Where is the duke? He's the one who should hear me speak.

We are standing in the duke's place; and we will hear you speal: Makes sure you speak honestly.

I will speak courageously, at least. But, oh, poor souls, Are you here looking for innocence from these cunning men? Say good bye to your justice! Is the duke gone? Then your cause is gone too. The duke is unjust, To reject your honest plea for justice, And put your trial in the hands of the villain That you came here to accuse.

This is the scoundrel; this is the man that I spoke of.

Why, you disrespectful and unholy friar, Is it not enough that you have bribed these women To accuse this honorable man, but, with foul language And to his very face, To call him a villain? And then suddenly to go from him To the duke himself, and accuse him with injustice? Take him away; to the torture chamber with him! We'll pull you apart Joint by joint, until we know his purpose. He calls us 'unjust'!

DUKE VINCENTIO

Be not so hot; the duke
Dare no more stretch this finger of mine than he
Dare rack his own: his subject am I not,
Nor here provincial. My business in this state
Made me a looker on here in Vienna,
Where I have seen corruption boil and bubble
Till it o'er-run the stew; laws for all faults,
But faults so countenanced, that the strong statutes
Stand like the forfeits in a barber's shop,
As much in mock as mark.

*Don't be so hasty; the duke
Doesn't dare to torturously stretch my finger
and more than he Dare stretch his own: I am not
just subject, Nor am I from his region. My
business in this state Made me an onlooker here
in Vienna, Where I have seen corruption boil
and bubble Until it runs over the edge of the
pot; laws for all sins, But sins supported by
authority, that the strong laws
Stand like the small list of penalties in a
barber's shop, As much a joke as a warning.*

ESCALUS

Slander to the state! Away with him to prison!

*He speaks slander against the government! Take
him away to prison!*

ANGELO

What can you vouch against him, Signior Lucio?
Is this the man that you did tell us of?

*What can you accuse him for, Mister Lucio?
Is this the man that you told us of?*

LUCIO

'Tis he, my lord. Come hither, goodman baldpate:
do you know me?

*That's him, my lord. Come here, goodman bald-head:
Do you know me?*

DUKE VINCENTIO

I remember you, sir, by the sound of your voice: I
met you at the prison, in the absence of the duke.

*I remember you, sir, by the sound of your voice: I
Met you at the prison, while the duke was away.*

LUCIO

O, did you so? And do you remember what you said of the duke?

Oh, did you? And do you remember what you said about the duke?

DUKE VINCENTIO

Most notedly, sir.

Quite well, sir.

LUCIO

Do you so, sir? And was the duke a fleshmonger, a
fool, and a coward, as you then reported him to be?

*Do you, sir? And was the duke a whore chaser, a
Fool, and a coward, as you claimed he was then?*

DUKE VINCENTIO

You must, sir, change persons with me, ere you make
that my report: you, indeed, spoke so of him; and
much more, much worse.

Sir, you must switch persons with me, before you claim
That I said that: you, in fact, spoke of him that way; and
Said much more, and much worse.

LUCIO
O thou damnable fellow! Did not I pluck thee by the
nose for thy speeches?

Oh, you sinful man! Did I not pull you by the
Nose for your words?

DUKE VINCENTIO
I protest I love the duke as I love myself.

I declare that I love the duke like I love myself.

ANGELO
Hark, how the villain would close now, after his
treasonable abuses!

Listen, how the villain concludes now, after his
Treason like abuse!

ESCALUS
Such a fellow is not to be talked withal. Away with
him to prison! Where is the provost? Away with him
to prison! lay bolts enough upon him: let him
speak no more. Away with those giglots too, and
with the other confederate companion!

A man like that is not to be talked with. Take him away
To prison! Where is the provost? Take him away
To prison! Put him in chains: he will
Speak no more. Take away those harlots too, and
With the other accomplice companion!

DUKE VINCENTIO
[To PROVOST] Stay, sir; stay awhile.

[To PROVOST] Hold on, sir; stay here awhile.

ANGELO
What, resists he? Help him, Lucio.

What's this, he's resisting arrest? Help take him
away, Lucio.

LUCIO
Come, sir; come, sir; come, sir; foh, sir! Why, you
bald-pated, lying rascal, you must be hooded, must
you? Show your knave's visage, with a pox to you!
show your sheep-biting face, and be hanged an hour!
Will't not off?

Come on, sir, come on, sir; come on, sir; foh,
sir! Why, you
Bald-headed, lying scoundrel, do you have to keep your
Face hidden? Show your beastly face, curse you!
Show your whore chasing face, and be sent to death in an hour!
Will this hood not come off?

Pulls off the friar's hood, and discovers DUKE

DUKE VINCENTIO
Thou art the first knave that e'er madest a duke.
First, provost, let me bail these gentle three.

Sneak not away, sir; for the friar and you
Must have a word anon. Lay hold on him.

LUCIO
This may prove worse than hanging.

DUKE VINCENTIO
[To ESCALUS] What you have spoke I pardon:
sit you down:
We'll borrow place of him.

Sir, by your leave.
Hast thou or word, or wit, or impudence,
That yet can do thee office? If thou hast,
Rely upon it till my tale be heard,
And hold no longer out.

ANGELO
O my dread lord,
I should be guiltier than my guiltiness,
To think I can be undiscernible,
When I perceive your grace, like power divine,
Hath look'd upon my passes. Then, good prince,
No longer session hold upon my shame,
But let my trial be mine own confession:
Immediate sentence then and sequent death
Is all the grace I beg.

DUKE VINCENTIO
Come hither, Mariana.
Say, wast thou e'er contracted to this woman?

ANGELO
I was, my lord.

VINCENTIO

You are the first scoundrel that ever created a duke where there was not one before. First, provost, let me free the kind Isabel, gentle Mariana, and good Friar Peter.

To LUCIO

Don't sneak away, sir; for the friar and you Must have a word later. Keep hold of him.

This may end up being worse than being executed.

[To ESCALUS] What you have said I will forgive: sit down:
I'll take Angelo's seat.

To ANGELO

Sir, excuse me,
Do you have either words, or cleverness, or audacity, That can still help you? If you do,
Tell it now, until my story is told,
And no longer hold back.

Oh, my respected lord,
I would be guiltier than I already am,
If I thought I could remain undeteced,
When I realize that your grace, like the power of god, Has noticed my crimes. Well then, good duke, Don't hold the trial of my dishonor any longer But instead let my trial be my own confession: Immediate punishment first and after that death Is all the favors I ask for.

Come here, Mariana.
Tell me, were you ever betrothed to this woman?

I was, my lord.

DUKE VINCENTIO
Go take her hence, and marry her instantly.
Do you the office, friar; which consummate,
Return him here again. Go with him, provost.

Go take her away, and marry her immediately.
Friar Peter, marry them; when it is finished,
Bring him back here. Go with him, provost.

Exeunt ANGELO, MARIANA, FRIAR PETER
and PROVOST

ESCALUS
My lord, I am more amazed at his dishonour
Than at the strangeness of it.

My lord, I am more amazed at his dishonor
Than at the strangeness of the situation.

DUKE VINCENTIO
Come hither, Isabel.
Your friar is now your prince: as I was then
Advertising and holy to your business,
Not changing heart with habit, I am still
Attorney'd at your service.

Come here, Isabel.
The friar who helped you is now the duke:
before I was Attentive and devoted to your
problem, And since I don't change my attitude
with my clothes, I am still dedicated to your
service.

ISABELLA
O, give me pardon,
That I, your vassal, have employ'd and pain'd
Your unknown sovereignty!

Oh, forgive me,
Because I, your servant, have employed and
troubled Your royalty unknowingly!

DUKE VINCENTIO
You are pardon'd, Isabel:
And now, dear maid, be you as free to us.
Your brother's death, I know, sits at your heart;
And you may marvel why I obscured myself,
Labouring to save his life, and would not rather
Make rash remonstrance of my hidden power
Than let him so be lost. O most kind maid,
It was the swift celerity of his death,
Which I did think with slower foot came on,
That brain'd my purpose. But, peace be with
him!
That life is better life, past fearing death,
Than that which lives to fear: make it your
comfort,
So happy is your brother.

You are forgiven, Isabel:
And now, dear lady, I hope you are as forgiving
to us. Your brother's death, I know, weighs on
your heart; And you may wonder why I
disguised myself, Working to save his life, and
didn't instead Hastily reveal my hidden power
Rather than let him be executed. Oh most kind
lady, It was because of the hurried speed of his
death, Which I thought was approaching slower,
That destroyed my plan. But, peace be with him!
That existence is a better life, beyond the fear of
death,
That the life that is lived in fear: comfort
yourself with that thought,
Your brother is content.

ISABELLA
I do, my lord.

I do, my lord.

Re-enter ANGELO, MARIANA, FRIAR PETER,
and PROVOST

DUKE VINCENTIO

For this new-married man approaching here,
Whose salt imagination yet hath wrong'd
Your well defended honour, you must pardon
For Mariana's sake: but as he adjudged your
brother,--
Being criminal, in double violation
Of sacred chastity and of promise-breach
Thereon dependent, for your brother's life,--
The very mercy of the law cries out
Most audible, even from his proper tongue,
'An Angelo for Claudio, death for death!'
Haste still pays haste, and leisure answers
leisure;
Like doth quit like, and MEASURE still FOR
MEASURE.
Then, Angelo, thy fault's thus manifested;
Which, though thou wouldst deny, denies thee
vantage.
We do condemn thee to the very block
Where Claudio stoop'd to death, and with like
haste.
Away with him!

MARIANA

O my most gracious lord,
I hope you will not mock me with a husband.

DUKE VINCENTIO

It is your husband mock'd you with a husband.
Consenting to the safeguard of your honour,
I thought your marriage fit; else imputation,
For that he knew you, might reproach your life
And choke your good to come; for his
possessions,
Although by confiscation they are ours,
We do instate and widow you withal,
To buy you a better husband.

MARIANA

O my dear lord,
I crave no other, nor no better man.

DUKE VINCENTIO

Never crave him; we are definitive.

As for this newly married man approaching us here, Whose lustful imagination would have wronged Your preserved honor, you must forgive him For Mariana's sake: but since he condemned your brother,--
And is therefore a criminal in violation of both Of taking a virgin and of breaking the promise On which that virginity depended, for your brother's life,-- The merciful nature of the law cries out Loudly, even from his own tongue, for 'Angelo for Claudio, a death for a death!' Speediness still repays speediness, and lenience repays lenience;
Like repays like, and always measure for measure.
Then, Angelo, your crime thus proven; Which, even if you were to deny it, it would do you no good.
We sentence you to the very same executioners block Where Claudio gave in to death, and with the same speediness.
Take him away!

Oh, my most gracious lord,
I hope you are not taunting me with a husband.

It is your husband who taunted you with a husband. As I agreed to protect your honor, I thought your marriage was acceptable; otherwise accusations, Because of your sexual relations with him, might condemn your life And strangle what good is to come to you; because his possessions, Although we confiscated them, We bequeath to you and give you a widow's settlement with that, To provide a dowry for a better husband.

Oh, my dear lord,
I want no other man, nor do I want a better man.

Don't want him; we have set our minds on this.

MARIANA
Gentle my liege,--

My gentle lord,--

Kneeling

DUKE VINCENTIO
You do but lose your labour.
Away with him to death!

You are wasting your efforts,
Take him away to death!

To LUCIO

Now, sir, to you.

Now, sir, on to you.

MARIANA
O my good lord! Sweet Isabel, take my part;
Lend me your knees, and all my life to come
I'll lend you all my life to do you service.

Oh, my good lord! Sweet Isabel, take my side;
Kneel with me, and for the rest of my life
I'll give you everything in my power to help you.

DUKE VINCENTIO
Against all sense you do importune her:
Should she kneel down in mercy of this fact,
Her brother's ghost his paved bed would break,
And take her hence in horror.

Completely unreasonably are you asking for her
help: Why should she kneel down for mercy of
this crime, Her brother's ghost would break out
of his grave, And take her away in horror.

MARIANA
Isabel,
Sweet Isabel, do yet but kneel by me;
Hold up your hands, say nothing; I'll speak all.
They say, best men are moulded out of faults;
And, for the most, become much more the better
For being a little bad: so may my husband.
O Isabel, will you not lend a knee?

Isabel,
Sweet Isabel, please just kneel by me;
Hold up your hands, you don't have to say
anything; I'll say everything. They say that the
best men are created out of their crimes; And,
for the most part, become so much better
Because they were a little bad: so it could be
with my husband. Oh, Isabel, won't you kneel
with me?

DUKE VINCENTIO
He dies for Claudio's death.

He dies for Claudio's death.

ISABELLA
Most bounteous sir,

Most giving sir,

Kneeling

Look, if it please you, on this man condemn'd,
As if my brother lived: I partly think
A due sincerity govern'd his deeds,
Till he did look on me: since it is so,

If you would like, consider this condemned man
The same as you would if my brother has lived: I
partly think A proper authenticity led him to do
what he did, Until he looked on me: since that's

140

Let him not die. My brother had but justice,
In that he did the thing for which he died:
For Angelo,
His act did not o'ertake his bad intent,
And must be buried but as an intent
That perish'd by the way: thoughts are no subjects;
Intents but merely thoughts.

MARIANA
Merely, my lord.

DUKE VINCENTIO
Your suit's unprofitable; stand up, I say.
I have bethought me of another fault.
Provost, how came it Claudio was beheaded
At an unusual hour?

PROVOST
It was commanded so.

DUKE VINCENTIO
Had you a special warrant for the deed?

PROVOST
No, my good lord; it was by private message.

DUKE VINCENTIO
For which I do discharge you of your office:
Give up your keys.

PROVOST
Pardon me, noble lord:
I thought it was a fault, but knew it not;
Yet did repent me, after more advice;
For testimony whereof, one in the prison,
That should by private order else have died,
I have reserved alive.

DUKE VINCENTIO
What's he?

PROVOST
His name is Barnardine.

DUKE VINCENTIO

the case, Do not have him die. My brother had only justice, In that he committed the crime for which he died: For Angelo,
The crime he intended was not carried out,
And must be forgotten as only an intention
That went by the wayside: thoughts are not people;
Intentions are only thoughts.

Only, my lord.

Your case won't work; stand up, I say.
I have thought of another crime.
Provost, why was Claudio beheaded
At an unusual hour?

I was ordered to be like that.

Did you have a special warrant to do that?

No, my good lord; it was by private message.

For that you are fired from your position:
Give me your keys.

Excuse me, noble lord:
I thought it was wrong, but I didn't know;
But I did regret it, after more consideration;
To testify to this there is someone in the prison,
Who should have also died by private order,
That I have kept alive.

Who's he?

His name is Barnardine.

I would thou hadst done so by Claudio.
Go fetch him hither; let me look upon him.

I wish you had done that for Claudio.
Go bring him here; let me look at him.

Exit PROVOST

ESCALUS
I am sorry, one so learned and so wise
As you, Lord Angelo, have still appear'd,
Should slip so grossly, both in the heat of blood.
And lack of temper'd judgment afterward.

I am sorry that someone so educated and so
wise As you, Lord Angelo, has still managed
To slip up so badly, both from the heat of sexual
desire, And from the lack of careful thought
afterward.

ANGELO
I am sorry that such sorrow I procure:
And so deep sticks it in my penitent heart
That I crave death more willingly than mercy;
'Tis my deserving, and I do entreat it.

I am sorry that I have created such sorrow;
And so it runs deep in my remorseful heart
That I would go to death more willingly than
receive mercy; It's what I deserve, and I ask for
it.

Re-enter PROVOST, with BARNARDINE,
CLAUDIO muffled, and JULIET

DUKE VINCENTIO
Which is that Barnardine?

Which of you is Barnardine?

PROVOST
This, my lord.

This one, my lord.

DUKE VINCENTIO
There was a friar told me of this man.
Sirrah, thou art said to have a stubborn soul.
That apprehends no further than this world,
And squarest thy life according. Thou'rt
condemn'd:
But, for those earthly faults, I quit them all;
And pray thee take this mercy to provide
For better times to come. Friar, advise him;
I leave him to your hand. What muffled fellow's
that?

There was a friar who told me about this man.
Man, you are said to have a stubborn soul.
That doesn't understand anything past his
world, And that you live your life accordingly.
You are comdemned:
But, for these mortal crimes, I forgive you;
And please take this mercy to provide for
yourself In better times to come. Friar, give him
guidance; I leave him in your hands. Who's that
concealed fellow?

PROVOST
This is another prisoner that I saved.
Who should have died when Claudio lost his
head;
As like almost to Claudio as himself.

This is another prisoner that I saved.
Who was supposed to have died when Claudio
lost his head;

As similar to Claudio as himself.

Unmuffles CLAUDIO

142

DUKE VINCENTIO

[To ISABELLA] If he be like your brother, for his sake
Is he pardon'd; and, for your lovely sake,
Give me your hand and say you will be mine.
He is my brother too: but fitter time for that.
By this Lord Angelo perceives he's safe;
Methinks I see a quickening in his eye.
Well, Angelo, your evil quits you well:
Look that you love your wife; her worth worth yours.
I find an apt remission in myself;
And yet here's one in place I cannot pardon.

You, sirrah, that knew me for a fool, a coward,
One all of luxury, an ass, a madman;
Wherein have I so deserved of you,
That you extol me thus?

LUCIO

'Faith, my lord. I spoke it but according to the trick. If you will hang me for it, you may; but I had rather it would please you I might be whipt.

DUKE VINCENTIO

Whipt first, sir, and hanged after.
Proclaim it, provost, round about the city.
Is any woman wrong'd by this lewd fellow,
As I have heard him swear himself there's one
Whom he begot with child, let her appear,
And he shall marry her: the nuptial finish'd,
Let him be whipt and hang'd.

LUCIO

I beseech your highness, do not marry me to a whore.
Your highness said even now, I made you a duke:
good my lord, do not recompense me in making me a cuckold.

DUKE VINCENTIO

Upon mine honour, thou shalt marry her.
Thy slanders I forgive; and therewithal

[To ISABELLA] If he is like your brother, for Claudio's sake
His crimes are forgiven; and, for you lovely sake, Give me your hand in marriage and say you will be my wife. He is my brother too: but there's a better time for that. From all this Lord Angelo think he's safe; I think I see a new light in his eyes. Well Angelo, your evil has left you well: Make sure that you love your wife; she is worth as much as you.
I find myself ready to forgive;
And yet there's someone here I cannot forgive.

To LUCIO

You, man, that thought I was a fool, a coward,
A lustful man, an ass, and a madman;
What have I done to you that deserved
For you to speak of me this way?

By heaven, my lord. I spoke that way as a Prank. If you want to hang me for it, you may; but I Would rather if you would like me to be whipped.

Whipped, first, sir, and executed after.
Declare it, provost, all over the city.
If there is any woman who has been wronged by this lustful fellow, As I have heard him say himself that there was one Whom he got pregnant, let her come forward, And he will marry her: the marriage ceremony complete, He will be whipped and executed.

I beg your highness, do not make me marry a whore.
Your highness said it just now, I made you a duke:
My good lord, do not pay me back by making me husband to an unfaithful life.

On my honor, you will marry her.
Your slander I will forgive; and along with them

Remit thy other forfeits. Take him to prison;
And see our pleasure herein executed.

LUCIO
Marrying a punk, my lord, is pressing to death,
whipping, and hanging.

DUKE VINCENTIO
Slandering a prince deserves it.

She, Claudio, that you wrong'd, look you
restore.
Joy to you, Mariana! Love her, Angelo:
I have confess'd her and I know her virtue.
Thanks, good friend Escalus, for thy much
goodness:
There's more behind that is more gratulate.
Thanks, provost, for thy care and secrecy:
We shill employ thee in a worthier place.
Forgive him, Angelo, that brought you home
The head of Ragozine for Claudio's:
The offence pardons itself. Dear Isabel,
I have a motion much imports your good;
Whereto if you'll a willing ear incline,
What's mine is yours and what is yours is mine.
So, bring us to our palace; where we'll show
What's yet behind, that's meet you all should
know.

*I forgive your other crimes. Take him to prison;
And see that our wishes are carried out.*

*Marrying a whore, my lord, is the same as
death, Whipping, and hanging.*

Slandering a duke deserves such a punishment.

Exit Officers with LUCIO

*Claudio, the woman that you wronged, make
sure you marry her.
Joy to you, Mariana! Love her, Angelo:
I have received her confession and know her
virtue. Thanks, my good friend Escalus, for your
great honor.
There's more to come that is more expressive of
my thanks. Thanks, provost, for your care and
secrecy: I will give you a position in a better
place. Forgive the man, Angelo, that brought to
your house The head of Ragozine instead of
Claudio's: The offence forgives itself. Dear
Isabel, I have a proposal that would greatly
benefit you; Which, if you'll listen willingly,
Would make what's mine yours, and what's
yours mine. So, accompany me to my palace;
where I'll show you What's still to come, that's
appropriate for all of you to know.*

Exeunt